MENNYMS
IN THE WILDERNESS

MENNYMS
IN THE WILDERNESS

Sylvia Waugh

RED FOX

A Red Fox Book

Published by Random House Children's Books
20 Vauxhall Bridge Road, London SW1V 2SA

A division of Random House UK Ltd
London Melbourne Sydney Auckland
Johannesburg and agencies throughout the world

Copyright © Sylvia Waugh 1994

1 3 5 7 9 10 8 6 4 2

First published in Great Britain by Julia MacRae 1994

Red Fox edition 1995

Set in Joanna 12/14 by Intype
Printed and bound in Great Britain by
Cox & Wyman Ltd, Reading, Berkshire

RANDOM HOUSE UK Limited Reg. No. 954009

ISBN 0 09 942421 5

CONTENTS

CONTENTS

For David, Peter and Vicky

I have spread my dreams under your feet;
Tread softly because you tread on my dreams.

The Wind Among the Reeds, W.B. Yeats

1

The Letter

22 Calder Park
Gillygate
Durham
10th August

Dear Family

This is the strangest and most difficult letter I have
ever had to write. It flies in the face of common sense.
If you are real people living at 5 Brocklehurst Grove,
you won't have a clue what I'm talking about. My
waste-paper bin is full of discarded efforts. More than
once, I decided to give up trying. But a promise to a
ghost is very compelling, even in the light of common
day. I have to keep telling myself that I did see a ghost
and I did make a promise.

I am an ordinary human being. In no way am I
special. But, if the things I have been told are true,
you will recognise my name. I was called after my
father. My name is Albert Pond. But I am not a mythical

Australian. I am English – and completely real! All of which takes a fair bit of explaining.

It began one day last week . . .

I was sitting on a bench by the river just above Prebends Bridge. I had been down in the depths of the library all morning, catching up on unfinished work. So it was a relief to come out for a breath of fresh air.

You must picture a steep grassy bank above me rising right up to the walls of the Cathedral. Beneath me there is a gritty path, more grass, and trees everywhere. The river below is barely visible. I am alone.

Then suddenly I am not alone. For the first time in my thirty years of life, I am about to see a ghost. It is a very weird experience. I have never even believed in ghosts before. First, I have the sense of there being someone close beside me. I look around. The path either side is deserted. The nearest human beings are on the bridge away to my left, not even within hailing distance. I look along the seat and there, hovering on my right, is what I can only describe as a swathe of grey smoke.

Everything around me becomes totally still. The leaves are not moving on the trees. There is no movement on the bridge. Everything is silent.

"Don't worry," says a firm voice out of the mist. "I won't take long."

Within seconds, there is no mist any more, just a real, very solid, elderly lady wearing a heather-coloured tweed jacket and skirt and a deep pink jumper. From her wiry grey hair, neatly bobbed, to her brown brogue shoes, she looks rather old-fashioned, but completely alive. Her sharp brown eyes are youthful.

Her broad, downy cheeks are the colour of ripe peaches, the lines on her face are faint and pleasant-looking.

"You won't know me," she says briskly, "but I know who you are. Your grandfather was my nephew. I am Kate Penshaw."

Then I realise with a shock that I have seen her before. She is in the family photograph album, holding my father on her knee when he was just two years old. I know it is the same woman, but if she were alive today she would have to be at least a hundred and ten.

"Why am I not afraid of you?" I ask. I feel genuinely puzzled and out of my depth.

"Why should you be?" asks Kate with just the glimmer of a smile.

"You are a ghost, aren't you?"

"If you say so," says Kate. "I am not at all sure what I am. I do know what I am here for."

Then she tells me all about the Mennyms, down to the last detail. She knows much more than you might think. She claims to have lived with you and through you since the day she died. She makes me believe her, even though the things she says are totally fantastic.

"And now," she says as she brings the story up to the present, "they are in danger of losing their home. For the first time in all these years, they are threatened from outside in a way that could lead to their destruction. The danger is, as yet, no bigger than a speck on the horizon. But I have been warned of it. And, to put it very simply, I am here because we need your help."

She clasps her hands together in her lap and leans towards me with a look of real anxiety.

"Do you understand?"

I don't. But, from habit, I nod as if I do. People explain things much better if you don't insist upon understanding every word they say.

"Plans are being made," she continues, "to pull down Brocklehurst Grove and to drive a motorway right through the house. And there's not a thing I can do about it. I haven't the power, not the power it would need to stop something as big as that."

I suddenly realise what she wants me for. And it chills me to the bone. I don't ask her any of the obvious questions as to where she has come from and what it is like there, or how she has managed to come back, or even how you people are so alive. Instead, I say, "I can't see what use I would be. I'm not in town-planning or anything like that. I wouldn't know where to start."

Aunt Kate looks relieved.

"That's no problem, Albert. I can tell you where to start. I didn't come here without considering what could be done. Write to them. Meet them. Give them a new home if need be. There is Comus House, remember. You hardly ever go there yourself. You might as well put it to some good use."

She fixes me with those sharp brown eyes and makes me promise to do all I can.

"You won't be alone," she says. "I'll be there in the background keeping an eye on things."

Then she gets up and walks quickly away along the river bank. She doesn't even dematerialise like a proper ghost. As for me, I just sit stunned as the leaves rustle in the breeze again and faint sounds of distant people and traffic reach my ears.

So now I am writing to warn you of what is going to happen, and, goodness knows how I'll do it, to offer you whatever help I can give. I still feel very unsure of some of the things Aunt Kate told me, but I'll be in an even worse muddle if I have to decide whether ghosts can tell lies. So all I can do is try to believe everything and act accordingly.

As far as I can make out, the motorway must still be in its very early planning stage. None of your neighbours will know anything about it yet. There is no desperate hurry. I have Kate's word for that. I already have a holiday arranged and she says it will be perfectly safe for me to go. I shall write again as soon as there is anything more to tell.

Take your time. Learn to live with the idea that there is one living human being who knows all about you but who will share that knowledge with no one. Aunt Kate was very firm on that point.

Yours sincerely,
Albert Pond

2

Not Again!

Albert Pond's letter arrived by the second delivery on Wednesday.

Life was being beautifully normal. Joshua Mennym was in the garden tidying the weeds and stopping occasionally to place one hand in the middle of his back as if it were beginning to ache. This backache was no more real than that of many another man, but the motives were not those of a malingerer. It was a nice simple pretend. It looked good. It felt good. Then he would take his large handkerchief out to wipe some non-existent sweat from his brow. Seen from the neighbouring houses which, thank goodness, were a decent distance away, he would look the genuine article – a middle-aged man keeping the garden in order. No one would suspect, no one had ever suspected, that the Mennyms were not human beings but living, intelligent, life-sized rag dolls. Of necessity, they kept themselves very strictly to themselves.

For over forty years the Mennyms had lived unknown and unnoticed at 5 Brocklehurst Grove. In all that time they had never grown any older; they had never been any younger. They had come mysteriously to life after their maker died, and they had managed miraculously to live together like any other family. All direct contact with the outside world was done by telephone, or by post. In the street, they kept their heads down and avoided being noticed with a skill that bordered on genius. Never in all those years had they spoken a word to the neighbours or even looked at them. To have done so would have been disastrous.

Poopie, Joshua's ten-year-old son, wheeled the barrow round the corner to gather up the rubbish. He enjoyed leaning heavily on the handles and taking a swift curving path to wherever he wanted to be. His twin sister, Wimpey, was sitting on the swing, watching them in a dreamy fashion, the swing barely moving. The sun shone on her golden curls and blue satin ribbons. She made a pretty picture that would grace any family album. So thought Granny Tulip, as she looked out of the breakfast-room window. She had the window wide open today and was busy sewing 'tulipmennym' labels into three jumpers that were just about ready for dispatch to the London store where they would be sold to the rich and the famous.

Joshua's wife, Vinetta, ever the busy mother, was in the kitchen putting sheets into the washing machine. It was not a job she enjoyed. The machine being a twin-tub, she had to transfer the wet load from one cylinder to the other. An automatic machine would have been more practical but that would have meant employing a plumber to instal it.

Upstairs, Granpa Mennym was writing a rather contentious article on the English Civil War. He was deeply engrossed. His purple foot, the one that could always be seen flopping over the side of his bed, felt as if it were booted and spurred. Books and magazines were strewn over his counterpane and tipping onto the floor.

Pilbeam and Appleby, the teenage daughters, were up in the latter's bedroom listening to pop music and looking at

17

magazines. Appleby's room was much bigger than Pilbeam's and the two often used it as a retreat. That was where they kept the stereo.

In the lounge, Soobie, the blue Mennym, was feeling even sadder than usual. Soobie was Pilbeam's twin brother, but unlike her, or any other member of the clan, he had a face that was entirely blue. His clothing was blue, his hands were blue and his feet were blue. Goodness knows why Kate made him that way. For, just like the rest of his family, he had been created by Kate Penshaw, a very clever needle-woman who had filled her home and the last years of her life with 'people' of her own making. A gloomy sense of foreboding hovered over Soobie. And that was even before the letter was opened.

Miss Quigley, the nanny, came up the front path with baby Googles in the pram. She let herself in with the key Vinetta had given her, a proud possession on an old key-ring with a picture of a cathedral embossed in the leather.

"You'd better have this, Hortensia," Vinetta had said. "It's not as if you were a visitor anymore. You live here now."

On this particular Wednesday morning as Miss Quigley pushed the pram into the hall and carefully removed her key from the lock, she looked down and saw the letter on the doormat.

She picked it up.

She looked at the address.

She sniffed.

"There's a letter here, Vinetta," she called.

"Who is it for?" asked Vinetta as she came out of the kitchen.

"Everybody," said Miss Quigley. "Everybody but me."

The letter was in fact addressed to 'The Mennym Family'.

It was in a long white envelope, but the address was handwritten.

"A personal letter," said Vinetta and then she shuddered. Mennyms never received personal letters. The only time they had ever done so was when Appleby had invented a character she called Albert Pond and had sneaked in letters supposed to come all the way from Australia.

"It's not from Australia," said Miss Quigley tactlessly.

"No, it's not," said Vinetta. She turned her back on Hortensia and didn't even bother to look at Googles.

I know my place, thought Miss Quigley. She's my friend when it suits her, but it doesn't suit her to open that letter in front of me. It's not even as if I am nosy. Let them keep their letters. I have more to think about.

"Come along, baby," she said to Googles as she lifted her out of the pram. "We'll go into the back garden this afternoon and you can watch me paint."

Vinetta looked at Hortensia and smiled a bit nervously. She did not want to upset her, but she needed to be alone to open that envelope.

"It's a lovely day," she said. "If I get the time I might just come out there and join you. I have worked quite hard this morning. I deserve a lazy afternoon."

Hortensia smiled back, totally undeceived. Googles wriggled about in her arms impatiently. She was always changed and fed and burped like any other baby, but it was all a pretend. There was never any milk in the bottle, and her nappy was always clean and dry. But she was a lively little one, well-loved and well-cared-for.

"I'd better go and settle her down," said Miss Quigley. "She probably needs changing. We've had a very long walk. The park was beautiful today."

3

Who?

"I don't know what to do about it," said Vinetta weakly as she sat with Granny Tulip in the breakfast-room. Both women had read the letter two or three times over.

"It sounds genuine," said Tulip.

"Anything Appleby writes sounds genuine. When it comes to fabricating lies she has no equal. It's almost as if she doesn't recognise the difference between fact and fiction."

"Put it this way," said Tulip, "if Appleby had not made up all that rubbish about Albert Pond coming on a visit from Australia, what would you have thought of this letter?"

"I'd have believed it. Naturally I would. That's why I really don't know what we should do."

"Besides," said Tulip shrewdly, "Appleby is very clever. I think she is too clever to play the same trick twice."

"Maybe you're right," Vinetta conceded, "but it could be a double bluff. I mean, if she did manage to fool us again that would be even more of a triumph."

"No," said Tulip, "I don't think she ever thought of it that way, Vinetta. You know she didn't. It was a game."

Vinetta turned the letter over helplessly. It was so difficult to know the truth. It would be so easy to jump to the wrong conclusion. That there should be two Albert Ponds, one fiction and Australian, the other fact and living not so very far away, was hard to swallow. And this new Albert Pond had a father who was also Albert Pond! It didn't bear thinking about.

"Well," said Tulip, ready as ever to push for a decision, "as I see it, we have various options open to us. We can tear the letter up and not even bother telling the others about it. But we can only do that if you feel absolutely sure that Appleby wrote it. Or we can confront Appleby in a quiet way and try to find out if she is guilty. Or we can hold a meeting and read the letter to all of them. Given the seriousness of the supposed threat, I think the last course is the safest. Let Magnus read it first and then we can have a conference in his room."

"Not a conference," said Vinetta sharply. "Remember what happened last time. I won't have it. If Appleby walks out, so do I. If she really wrote this letter, she must be sick."

"What do you mean to do then? Ignore the letter?" said Tulip. "Throw it away and forget about it? She's your daughter. Are you so sure that she is the culprit?"

"Let me have another look at the envelope," said Vinetta. "It might give us some clue."

They both looked at the stamp and the smudged circular postmark. The letter had been franked in Durham on Tuesday morning.

"Are you sure?" asked Tulip, peering closely through her little round spectacles.

"Of course I'm sure," said Vinetta. "You can make it out quite clearly."

"Then Appleby can't have posted it. It must be genuine."

"Unless she's forged the postmark," Vinetta pointed out.

21

"If she can produce airmail letters from anywhere in the world, a letter from Durham would be simple."

"So we are back to where we started," said Tulip. "We must simply weigh the probabilities."

"The only thing I do know," said Vinetta, "is that there is to be no confrontation. I won't have it."

Tulip looked annoyed.

"If it is genuine, and I tend to think it is, then we have more to worry about than upsetting Appleby. Honestly, Vinetta, we can't just leave it. We have to get at the truth."

At that moment, Pilbeam came into the breakfast-room.

"Are you two arguing again?" she asked, looking from her mother to her grandmother. She was never as impertinent as Appleby but she tended to regard her elders with a certain amusement that just stopped short of insolence.

Tulip looked haughty and Lady-Mennymish. Vinetta, ever peaceable, said, "Not exactly. Maybe you can help us out."

She handed Pilbeam the letter.

"She shouldn't read it before Magnus and Joshua," said Tulip. "It's not right."

The other two ignored her and Pilbeam read on with growing surprise.

"Well," she said, "that's the oddest thing I've ever heard."

"Who wrote it?" demanded Tulip.

"Who?" queried Pilbeam, her black eyes turned sharply on her grandmother. "Albert Pond, of course. That is what it says in the letter."

"Not Appleby?" Vinetta asked, looking hopefully at the daughter who had done so much for the delinquent Appleby over the past year. Pilbeam smiled back.

"No," she said, "not Appleby."

"Are you sure?" her mother insisted.

"Ninety-nine per cent sure," said Pilbeam.

"Not a hundred per cent?"

"It is hard to be a hundred per cent sure. Though really, we'd be better off if it were Appleby. You have odd priorities, Mum. We're going to lose this house. We look like making our first direct contact with a human being who knows all about us. And all you're worried about is whether Appleby is at the bottom of it. I'm sure she's not, but I wish she were."

Tulip gave Pilbeam a look of approval.

"Besides," said Pilbeam, light dawning as she recalled things Appleby had told to her and her alone, "I remember Appleby telling me where she found the name Albert Pond."

"She didn't invent it?" asked Vinetta.

"No," said Pilbeam. "She found it written inside the cover of an old book in her room. There definitely has been a real Albert Pond at some time. There could well be one now."

"So what do we do next?" said Tulip, a question addressed more to herself than to either of the others, but it was Pilbeam who answered.

"We have a meeting, of course. Don't we always?"

Tulip was not sure whether this was meant as sarcasm or not, but she let it pass.

"We'll have to answer Albert Pond's letter," continued Pilbeam, "and we'll have to face up to everything he's told us. There's not much choice."

Vinetta stood up and made for the door.

"If there is a meeting to be held," she said coldly, "I am going to make sure that Appleby is not upset by it. Give me the letter."

"And when do Magnus and Joshua get to read it, I'd like to know," said Tulip. "You'll be asking Miss Quigley to read it to Googles next! Pilbeam is right, Vinetta. You have very odd priorities."

23

Vinetta took the letter from Pilbeam and went out, slamming the door behind her in a most uncharacteristic manner.

Vinetta knocked gently, almost timidly, at Appleby's door and waited to be invited in.

"What are you waiting outside for? The door's open. Do you want a red carpet or something?"

Vinetta sighed. When Appleby was irritable, she was very, very irritable. Vinetta went in and closed the door behind her.

"We've had a letter," she began, wondering how to avoid sounding suspicious.

"What's that to me?" asked her daughter in a sulky voice. Pop music was still blaring from the stereo. Vinetta, taking her life in her hands, went and turned it off before seating herself in the chair beside the bed where Appleby lay sprawled out and surrounded by magazines.

"I sent Pilbeam down for a pair of scissors. Where is she? It shouldn't have taken her all this long!"

"Pilbeam is in the breakfast-room with your grandmother. And I doubt very much if you sent her there," said Vinetta. "It's Pilbeam you're talking about, remember. She's not at your beck and call, and well you know it."

Appleby drew a strand of red hair across her mouth, looked cheeky and said nothing.

"This letter," Vinetta continued. "It is from one of Aunt Kate's relatives — a distant relative who, I suppose, must possess some psychic powers."

That struck the right chord. Appleby looked more interested. She and Pilbeam were into psychic powers at the moment, having a go at telepathy, and trying to move concrete objects by mental effort. They had not met with success in either field, but they hadn't given up yet.

"He must be psychic if he knows about us," she said with her usual acuteness.

"Well, he does," said her mother emphatically. "He knows all about us, every single thing."

Appleby looked even more interested.

"And you mean to say he's a real human being?"

"I've just told you. What else could he be? He's Kate's nephew. I don't know how far removed, but that's what he is. She has spoken to him."

"But she's dead," said Appleby. "She's been dead for over forty years. We all know that."

"You have heard of ghosts," said her mother. "Why do you think I said he must be psychic?"

Appleby's eyebrows rose an inch. Her green eyes looked larger and wider.

"Wow!" she said. "This man's seen Aunt Kate's ghost? I wish I'd been there. I wish I'd seen her. Give me that letter."

Appleby snatched the pages from Vinetta's hand and began to read. Vinetta watched her anxiously. She had hoped to prepare her for the young man's name before handing over the letter.

"Albert Pond!" shrieked her daughter as she came to the dreaded name. "Albert Pond! How dare you? What a horrible joke! Get out of my room. I never want to see you again. You're twisted."

Indignation from Appleby on this scale was rich. She should have been the last person to be so disgusted at a hoax, even if it was a hoax.

Vinetta didn't rise from her chair, though for a minute it even looked as if Appleby might hit her. It was not something that Appleby had ever done before. It would have been totally out of character. But the temptation was there. She was truly furious.

"You didn't give me time to warn you," said her mother in as soothing a voice as she could manage. "But the young man puts it clearly enough. He can't help his name."

Appleby still looked wild. Vinetta took hold of her wrist and gripped it tightly.

"Read the letter, Appleby," she said gently, "all of it. You're cleverer than the rest of us. We're hoping you'll be able to help us decide what to do."

Appleby looked at her unbelievingly.

"It's not a joke then?"

"Of course it's not," said Vinetta. "Do you seriously think I'd be party to a cruel, nasty joke like that? I thought at first that you – well, you did do it before . . ." she faltered.

Appleby read the whole of the letter.

"Has Granpa seen it yet?" she asked when she had finished reading.

"No," said Vinetta firmly. Now that the storm was over she felt more sure of what to say. "I wanted you to see it first. After all, he is going to think that you wrote it. No good getting uppity! It's what they'll all think, given your past record."

"Do you think I wrote it?" asked Appleby suspiciously.

"I did at first. Anybody would."

"And you are sure now that it wasn't me?" Appleby repeated looking at her closely.

"Ninety-nine per cent sure," said her mother, using Pilbeam's words.

"And when will you be a hundred per cent sure?" demanded Appleby.

Vinetta hadn't considered this.

"When we meet the real Albert Pond, I suppose. Till then we don't really know anything for certain."

"Of course," said Appleby, "it could be one of the others.

It could be somebody's idea of a joke, even if it wasn't yours."

"Whose?"

Appleby considered carefully. The older Mennyms were out of the question. Poopie might be guilty, but he wasn't clever enough. Neither was Wimpey, but she wouldn't want to be so mischievous. Pilbeam and Soobie were both clever but neither of them would indulge in such a fanciful pretend.

"What about Miss Quigley?" asked Appleby at last. "She's always been jealous, you know, because she is not a Mennym. There are lots of stories about evil nannies."

"Appleby Mennym! That's a dreadful thing to say," said Vinetta. "Hortensia Quigley wouldn't harm anybody. She is too much of a lady. You change your tune when it suits you. Remember how indignant you and Pilbeam were when Hortensia was living in the cupboard and pretending to have a house in Trevethick Street?"

"That was different," said Appleby. "We thought she was helpless and pathetic. But she's not."

"I should think not," said Vinetta. "She is the best nanny anyone could wish for."

Soobie

The family conference was delayed. Sir Magnus decided to have 'the gout'. This was a grandiose pretend that affected his right foot, the one that was always well hidden under the counterpane. When 'the gout' came on, Tulip would place a wicker frame under the top sheet to protect the inflamed big toe that was presumably becoming uncomfortably distended.

The letter from Albert Pond was the cause of it all. Granpa Mennym had not a single pearl of wisdom to fit this occasion. It was no good saying "Least said, soonest mended," or "Everything comes to him who waits." It did occur to him that "Better the devil you know than the devil you don't" might be vaguely applicable, but only as a witty reference to Appleby who, even after all her mischief, was still the old man's favourite. (It was some time since Appleby had indulged her idle fancy by inventing the Australian Albert Pond. The pain of all that followed was beginning to dim. Old men forget.) Then again, this new Albert Pond, whoever he was, had told them to take their time. That was one piece of advice Magnus felt free to follow.

August gave way to September. Everyone in the house,

including Miss Quigley, knew about the letter and had had time to think about it. Poopie stopped speaking to Appleby. Appleby tossed her head whenever she passed Miss Quigley in the hall or on the stairs. Tulip even found herself looking suspiciously at her husband and wondering if elderly rag dolls could, to put it kindly, become mentally unbalanced. Magnus was easily as clever as Appleby, so she thought. He could have coaxed Joshua to be his accomplice. No! Don't be stupid! Joshua would run a mile from anything as fanciful as that!

Soobie was only eighty per cent sure that Appleby had not written the letter. No further letters had arrived. But then this Albert Pond, if indeed it were Albert Pond, had said they should take their time. Nor had he said how long his holiday would be.

"Do you think there really is an Albert Pond?" Wimpey asked Soobie one sunny afternoon. She had played all morning in the garden and had decided to come into the lounge and sit by the fire, pretending it was winter again. Soobie did not need to pretend. All seasons were alike and daytime was chair-time and night-time was bedtime. He looked up from the book he was reading.

"You'd better ask Appleby," he said sourly. "I don't know what to believe."

Wimpey was sitting on the hearth rug with her feet tucked under her. She looked up at her older brother and struggled to think. If Soobie did not know the answer, it must be a hard problem.

"If you wrote a letter to Albert Pond," she said at last, "and nobody else knew and I sneaked out and put it in the post-box, and he wrote back, then we would know he was real. Well, we would, wouldn't we?"

Soobie looked at his little sister. There she was, forever

ten years old, her golden hair in bunches, her pale blue eyes eternally innocent, and she had come up with the perfect answer. Only she might tell Poopie, and Poopie might tell Father and, oh what a household it was for being unable to keep a secret! A secret is only a secret if it is shared with no one.

"I'll think about it," said Soobie, lolling back in his chair. "It's a lovely day. Why don't you go out and play in the garden?"

Wimpey looked crestfallen. It had seemed such a good idea, but if Soobie wasn't keen, it mustn't be.

As soon as he was alone, Soobie sprang into action. Tulip was upstairs, tidying the big bedroom and being solicitous about 'the gout'. The plump blue Mennym went with unwonted speed into the breakfast-room and helped himself to a sheet of paper, an envelope and a stamp. There was a moment of panic when the brass bell fell to the floor, knocked over by a clumsy elbow. Soobie silently put it back on the desk. Then he went to his own room and wrote the letter with his own blue pen.

5th September

Dear Albert Pond,

You must write to me swiftly and personally if we are to believe that you exist. I have deliberately put no address at the top of this letter. If you are real, you will know where I live. I cannot risk any information falling into the hands of some mischievous stranger. One mischievous sister is more than enough for any R.D. And if you are real, you will know what those initials stand for.

Soobie M.

Just after midnight, when everyone in the house was sleeping, a hooded figure muffled in a winter coat stole out of the front door of 5 Brocklehurst Grove. A wind had sprung up that was strong enough to make the wintry attire unobtrusive should any passer-by notice him. But there was not a soul in sight.

It was Soobie. He had the letter in his pocket. He was born knowing where the letterboxes were, though he had never posted a letter before. He went left out of the Grove towards the three churches and the park. On the corner of a side street, just behind the first church, there was a remarkable letterbox, one of the few left in the country bearing the monogram of Queen Victoria. Soobie completed his task and returned home.

"Where on earth have you been at this time of night?" demanded Granny Tulip in a low, urgent voice as he passed the open door of the breakfast-room. He might have known! Granny was awake at all hours, knitting and watchful, more watchful than ever since the arrival of Albert's letter.

"I have been to post a letter," said Soobie tersely.

"At this time of night?" Tulip looked at him suspiciously.

"A blue Mennym could hardly go posting letters in the middle of the day," retorted Soobie.

"And where might you be sending letters to? Or is that too much to ask?" His grandmother's tone was sharp.

"Yes, it is," said Soobie. "I am tired. I am going to bed. And I am not going to answer any more questions."

5

Another Conference

There was a conference. There had to be a conference. In Granpa's room. Where else? It was held on a Tuesday evening so that Joshua could be present.

They all sat in their usual places. Only Googles was missing. She was safely tucked up in the day nursery. Miss Quigley had slid into the meeting last, after settling her charge down. She closed the door quite elegantly and sat on a stiff-backed chair. She really was different these days. There was no twittering apology for being late. A look in her eyes warned Sir Magnus to make no remark on her lateness and he didn't.

"Now that we are all here," he said without a trace of sarcasm in his voice, "it is time we sorted out what to do about Albert Pond's letter, whoever this Albert Pond may be. We cannot go on ignoring it indefinitely."

"We might as well," said Appleby. "It's obviously somebody's idea of a joke, and a pretty sick one at that."

She glared at Miss Quigley. In the last fortnight she had watched that lady very closely. It was certainly not the same Hortensia Quigley as the one who had once lived in the cupboard. It was not just the way she had become an expert on childcare, nor even the fact that she painted so beautifully.

32

She had just about stopped fluttering. She didn't apologise any more. She was cool, really cool. That was the word for it. Cool enough to take her revenge by inventing an Albert Pond more deadly than the last. At least the Australian had never threatened their home with demolition!

Miss Quigley glared back. She could feel the warmth of embarrassment in her cheeks. She could feel the flutter of her former self trying to get out, but she kept it firmly under control.

"We all know," she said acidly, "which member of this household is most inclined to play practical jokes."

What was good to give was certainly bad to take! Appleby stood up sharply, nearly tipping over her stool. "How dare you!" she said. "How dare you!"

"Keep calm," said Vinetta. "There is no point in anyone being suspicious of anyone else. I think this letter is perfectly genuine."

"I wrote it," said Poopie, with a wicked grin. "I wrote it all by myself. Hector showed me how to do it."

He giggled a bit nervously, suddenly realising that it was the wrong time for a joke.

"Hector couldn't show you anything," protested Wimpey. "He's just an Action Man."

"Be quiet, you two," said Tulip, with a careful eye to her husband who was obviously getting worked up and ready to let rip.

Granpa Mennym scowled. "If the younger members of this family cannot behave themselves," he said, "they will have to leave the room. What on earth are we coming to?"

"Sorry, Granpa," said Poopie.

"Sorry, Granpa," said Wimpey fervently, though she had less reason to apologise.

Appleby flopped down on her stool again and said

nothing. Pilbeam, seated on the floor beside her, gave her a look of sympathy. Appleby, she thought, was too complicated for her own good. There was a lot to be said for simplicity.

"What do you think we should do, Granpa?" asked Pilbeam, looking at her grandfather earnestly. Sir Magnus returned the look with one of solemn approval. Appleby would always be his favourite, but Pilbeam was much easier to live with!

"There is only one way," he said, "that we can be sure that Albert Pond is a real person living in a real house in Durham. I must write him a letter. Vinetta must post it because she is above suspicion. She will take this letter to the post after I have written it and sealed it. I alone will know what is in it. Any reply that comes will, at my request, contain clear evidence that the writer has read my words."

"'That's what I said," Wimpey chirped up excitedly. "That's what I told Soobie to do but he wouldn't listen."

"What do you mean?" asked Granpa, not quite following her words. "What did you tell him to do?"

"Write a secret letter to Albert Pond," said Soobie. "And I did do it. I did it two days ago. If he is real, there should be a reply as soon as he comes home from his holiday."

Granpa looked peeved. The blue Mennym had stolen his thunder. It was a very irritating pearl of wisdom to spring to mind just at that moment.

Joshua had sat silent the whole time. Now was his chance to say the only words he ever wanted to say at conference time.

"Well, that's that then. If Soobie's already written a letter, there's no need for us to do anything else."

He stood up and opened the door, giving the signal that the meeting was over.

6

Albert Comes Home

When Albert returned to his little house in Calder Park after an ill-fated holiday in Europe, he found *seven* letters and a postcard on the doormat.

The letters weren't all from Brocklehurst Grove, of course. One was from the University Library reminding him that his books were overdue. Another was from Castledean Council. The rest, with one exception, were from Mennyms.

Dear Mr Pond, (said the exception)

You may not have heard of me. I am not strictly speaking one of the Mennym family, though I do live in their household. I am nanny to Baby Googles. In most respects I am accepted as an honorary member of the family. Vinetta is my employer, but she insists upon my calling her by her first name and most of the time treats me as a dear friend.

It was, as you may imagine, with no little trepidation that we read your fascinating letter. We all look forward to meeting you at some convenient future date. In the meantime, I would like to use my small talent on your behalf, if you will permit. I am an artist. Mostly I paint still-life and landscapes, but I have done the occasional portrait and I would be honoured if you would send me a photograph that I could reproduce in oils for you. I have a medium-sized wood frame that is very nicely carved and gilded. It would be ideal for a portrait.

As to the threat to our home, I feel sure that you will be able to persuade the authorities to build their road elsewhere. Brocklehurst Grove is quite old and, in its quaint way, rather beautiful. I look forward to hearing from you.

Yours most sincerely,

Hortensia Quigley

It was a clever letter, or so thought its writer. If this Albert Pond existed, it would be a good thing to have a picture of him to check against any original that might appear. If he did not exist, then presumably the address in Calder Park would also be bogus.

Dear Mr Pond, (wrote Sir Magnus)

Your letter came as rather a shock. It is a good job I have a strong constitution. A less robust man of my age would surely have collapsed under the strain of it.

It seems to me, however, on reading and re-reading what you have to say, that the problem we have to face has not materialised yet. I have received no letters from the Council. There have been no notices in the press. None of our neighbours has tried to contact us, which surely in this extreme they would have done.

So at the moment all we need to do is maintain contact in case the worst should occur. Please write to confirm this.

I am, as you may know, a writer myself. I have evolved a somewhat complex filing system. To assist in filing your reply, I would appreciate it if you would write the following words as a postscript: 'Great is Diana of the Ephesians'.

With sincere regards,

Magnus Mennym

Of course the tale about the filing system was pure invention, as eccentric as the old man himself, though not in the same class as Appleby's. It was much more transparent and crudely naive.

Appleby's letter was surprisingly straightforward.

Dear Albert, (it read)

This is a simple request from a very simple person. Please make no further reference to your namesake in Australia. That episode is finished. No one mentions it anymore. It is an extremely delicate subject.

I must say how much I envy you your encounter with the ghost of Aunt Kate. I am rather psychic myself. The spirits of the past that hover round this house often make their presence felt to me. I have never mentioned this to any of the family. They would not understand. They are so extremely earthbound. Perhaps when you visit us we could hold a seance. I have this deep feeling that you will be the bringer of good fortune. No evil will touch this house once you have crossed its threshold.

I am,

Your kindred spirit,

Appleby Mennym

She had been tempted to write more. The prophetic flow was hard to resist, but the feeling that the sublime could become ridiculous acted as a curb.

Dear Albert, (wrote Pilbeam in her brief note)

Please, please be careful what you say about the other Albert Pond. If you really know everything about that matter, you could seriously upset Appleby. She has told some awful lies in her time, and will probably tell more, but she is deeply sensitive all the same, and more easily hurt than the rest of us.

Yours,

Pilbeam

And finally . . .

On the back of the picture postcard showing Castledean on market day, Wimpey had written:

> This is our town. Do you like the marketplace?
> Poopie and Wimpey Mennym

"There," said Wimpey. "Now he'll have to reply. We've asked him a question."

Poopie didn't answer.

"Well he will, won't he?" persisted Wimpey.

"I suppose so," said Poopie, though he wasn't really interested.

Castledean Council had written to tell Albert that if he had an interest in the property known as 5 Brocklehurst Grove, there was no reason from the planning point of view why he should not proceed with the purchase. No plans affecting this property were envisaged at present. Someone in Castledean Town Hall was adept at writing with his fingers crossed. True, the motorway was not strictly speaking a matter of town-planning. It was part of a national programme. True, the final plans had not reached the council offices yet. But a straight road beginning due east of the Grove and continuing due west was certainly on some secret agenda. Aunt Kate knew, and so did the 'someone' with his fingers crossed.

7

A Letter from Albert

22 Calder Park
Gillygate
Durham
14th October

Dear Family,

I am sorry it has taken me so long to write to you. I
omitted to mention, in my first letter, how long my
holiday was to be. In fact, I have only just returned,
having spent a fortnight in Paris, a week in Florence
and a week and a half in Rome. I didn't get to Naples,
or I might have been away even longer. But more of
that later . . .

Aunt Kate did tell me to enjoy my holiday. She did
not tell me how difficult it would be to put her out
of my mind. I kept imagining I could see her round
every corner. In Paris, for example, I went with my
friends to the Louvre. And there, standing in front of
a painting by Poussin, was a woman who could easily

have been Aunt Kate. For a split second I thought it was!

I went on to Florence alone. I was coming out of a dark little souvenir shop near the Duomo. The sun dazzled my eyes and I bumped into a tweedy woman who said briskly, "Mind how you go, young man." The voice was near enough the same to give me goose-flesh, for all the heat.

In Rome I met up with some friends from the University and everything was fun till the Wednesday of the second week. We were walking in a busy street near the Castel Sant'Angelo bridge when it happened.

It was another brilliant, hot sunny day. There we were strolling along. Then suddenly on the other side of the roadway, I caught sight of another 'Aunt Kate' dressed in the usual tweeds, her only concession to the weather being a frilly white blouse instead of the woollen jumper. I stared at her. I couldn't help it. Then all at once a policeman in a splendid white uniform was furiously blowing a whistle at me. At me?

One of our group yelled, "You can't cross there, Albert."

But I had crossed. I had a slow-motion collision with a fast-moving Fiat. It was a simple accident, but what followed, including my fractured leg, was terrifyingly complicated.

My left leg is now in plaster from the heel-bone to the thigh and will be for some weeks yet.

If all this does not prove to you that I am more than a bit inept on the practical side, I don't know what will. I wish Aunt Kate had been able to find a better champion for your cause. Still, I am willing to do whatever I can. For the moment, that is very little. Till my leg is out of plaster, I am pretty well useless.

There is one crumb of comfort I can offer you. If Aunt Kate is right about the motorway, she has obviously received the warning well in advance. The town-planners at Castledean know nothing about it. I pretended I was interested in buying your house and wrote for information about it before my holiday. I enclose their reply.

The photograph of myself is for Miss Quigley. It was taken three years ago, but I don't think I have changed very much since. Tell Appleby my lips are sealed, and Pilbeam need not worry either, assure Soobie that I am as real as anybody, and thank Poopie and Wimpey for the picture of Castledean market-place. When I am able to, I shall be delighted to pay you all a visit.

Kind regards to all,

Albert

P.S. Don't worry about me. I have friends who come in every day to help and a lady called Mrs Briggs comes three times a week to do the housework.
P.P.S. Great is Diana of the Ephesians.

8

Some Truth, Some Lies

A conference was held that very day. Sir Magnus was eager to see everybody as soon as possible. The afternoon sun was streaming in through the net curtains. On the whole, Granpa preferred the solemnity of an evening meeting, but it was Wednesday and Joshua would be going off to work.

All of the grown-ups in the family contributed to the household economy. Sir Magnus wrote articles on various subjects, but principally the English Civil War. He also composed crossword puzzles under the pseudonym *Magnopere*. Lady Tulip's knitwear, trade-name *tulipmennym*, was sold exclusively to Harrods. Vinetta was content to sell the children's clothes she made so beautifully to a local shop with some pretensions to being a boutique. Most of the business side was done by telephone and post and the proprietor, Cynthia Macaulay, held her lovely head so self-consciously high that she never looked closely at anyone, let alone the 'little woman' who delivered stock.

Joshua was the only one who had a real job that took him out of the house and into a workplace for five nights of the week. He was nightwatchman at Sydenham's Electrical Warehouse, a job he dearly loved. Every night except Tuesday and Saturday, he walked the three miles to work, all muffled up. He accepted the keys from Max, the dull-witted, dim-sighted labourer who stayed behind to sweep the floors. In the morning he handed them over to Charlie who always arrived first. Sneaking out before Charlie could look him in the face was an art he had perfected over many years.

"I don't mind if you have a conference without me, Father," Joshua had protested on this occasion as on many others. What he really meant was — please have your conference without me. I hate conferences and I prefer not to have my say, if that's what you're thinking.

"You're entitled to have your say," said the old man, though he knew perfectly well how Joshua felt. "It's only right and proper."

So there they all were, with varying degrees of enthusiasm or reluctance, gathered round the great man in the great bed, giving weighty consideration to Albert's letter.

"Now, who else has been writing to Kate's great-nephew?" Sir Magnus looked balefully at each in turn.

"We didn't know for sure that you had written," Soobie pointed out, "and everyone knew that I had."

"Pilbeam?" Her grandfather looked at her directly.

"Well, yes, I did write a note. No harm in that, I hope." There was something so self-possessed about Pilbeam that Granpa asked no more.

"And what about that picture he's sent for you, Miss Quigley?" he asked.

Miss Quigley felt a bit flustered but she controlled it. She controlled it! Control had become a habit.

"I suppose Aunt Kate must have told him that I was a painter in my own small way," she lied. "It might be his way of asking for a portrait."

"Hmmph," grunted Sir Magnus. "Bit too subtle for me. Still, it does give us a chance to have a look at the fellow."

The photograph was passed round. It showed a young man in an academic gown. His hair was light brown and wavy. His face was rather long and pale. His eyes were his most remarkable feature. They were very round, very dark and very wide-open so that he looked childlike and rather startled.

"A poor reed, that one," commented Granny Tulip. "He can't look after himself, never mind trying to look after anyone else!"

When everyone had finished examining the photograph, Miss Quigley retrieved it and slipped it into the pocket of her cardigan.

"Why," said Sir Magnus, returning to his questioning, "does he tell you that his lips are sealed, Appleby? What have you been saying this time?"

"That's right," said Appleby sharply, "go on, jump to conclusions. And be wrong as usual. As a matter of fact, I have never written him a letter. I didn't think it was worth it. Soobie had already sent his. I can only think that Albert Pond is, as I am, telepathic. Thought waves transmitted by me have reached his consciousness. He assumes that I do not wish anyone to be aware of my psychic powers."

The lie saved Appleby from having to explain why Albert's lips were sealed, but, more than that, she enjoyed telling it.

Sir Magnus gave her a shrewd look, but satisfied himself with saying, "Bunkum! Total bunkum!"

"You see," said Appleby, undeterred, "that is the normal reaction of the world to those of us who have the gift."

"Chuck it, Appleby," said Soobie. "We don't believe you and we're not impressed. Do you think we're stupid? We know you wrote to him."

"Poopie and me sent Albert Pond a postcard," chimed in Wimpey, "and he must have got it, mustn't he? He mentions it in his letter right at the end."

"Yes, sweetheart," said Vinetta, putting an arm round her daughter's shoulders, "that was very nice of you."

Poopie looked up from under his fringe.

"I want to ask something," he said.

"Well, go ahead. Ask," said Granpa indulgently.

"Who is Diana of the whatsit?"

"That, my boy," said Granpa, "is what is known as a coded message."

"But what does it mean?" Poopie looked stubborn.

"It doesn't have to mean anything," said Granpa flatly. "It is just a password proving that Albert Pond has received and read my letter. Any more questions?"

Sir Magnus glowered round the room as only he could glower.

"You know what the best bit of this letter is?" demanded Tulip.

"Come on then, tell us," said her husband, relieved to change the subject. The password sounded silly to him now and he found himself in the very unusual position of feeling embarrassed.

"There is no motorway planned for our part of Castledean. Aunt Kate must have been mistaken. We can stop worrying." That said, Tulip went on with her knitting.

"I don't know," said Magnus. "I don't trust planners. Today's truth is tomorrow's fiction. And in the meantime, what do we do about Albert Pond?"

"Send him a get-well card," said Soobie drily. "There's not much else you can do for the moment."

Appleby got away with being cheeky because she was Appleby, the apple of her grandfather's eye. Soobie got away with it because Magnus was never totally sure whether he was being cheeky or not.

Joshua heard the silence that followed Soobie's words and he breathed a sigh of relief. The meeting was surely over. There was nothing more to be said.

"He must be quite a wealthy young man," commented Tulip as she stood up and gathered her knitting into its bag. "A holiday like that must have cost him a fortune."

"No, he's not," said Appleby quickly. "He was saving up to get married and his girlfriend went off with somebody else. So he spent all he had on the holiday."

"And how do you know that, pray?" asked Granpa. "Telepathy, I suppose?"

Appleby looked baffled. She gave a very convincing shiver. "I don't know," she said. "I really don't know."

Soobie, the sceptical blue Mennym, gave her a searching look. This born-knowing business was something he had never been able to get used to. It was certainly a hindrance when it came to sifting truth from lies.

"I'm going to bed," said Joshua abruptly. "I can have a two hour nap before I get ready for work. We've said all there is to say for now, haven't we?"

Albert Speaks

The months passed. Albert received a charming get-well card from the whole family, a scatter of Christmas cards, and even an anonymous Valentine sent by Pilbeam and Appleby just for fun. He in turn sent them a progress report on the leg when it came out of plaster, and an old-fashioned glossy Christmas card with an embossed picture of a fat robin redbreast perched on a sprig of holly.

The motorway project remained under wraps for such a long time that they all began to believe Aunt Kate had made a mistake.

Then one day towards the end of March the telephone rang.

"Hello, hello," said a worried voice.

"Who is that?" demanded Sir Magnus. There were two telephones in the house, one in the breakfast-room and one on Granpa's bedside table.

"It's me," said the voice. "Albert Pond. I had to phone. Is that Sir Magnus?"

"You've never phoned before," said Magnus suspiciously, listening hard for any indication that this masculine voice was just a disguise put on by a female of the household. "Is that you, Appleby?"

Albert Pond tried desperately to sound convincing.

"Of course it's not," he said. "I'm Albert. You know — Kate's great-nephew. From Durham."

Silence.

"Great is Diana of the Ephesians," Albert added, thinking the old man might recognise this reference to his filing system.

"Well, if you really are you, what do you want?" demanded Sir Magnus. He wished he had never thought of using a password, particularly such a silly one. Was it going to haunt him forever?

"I had to phone you," said Albert. "There's something in this morning's papers about the motorway. It is definitely going to be built and Brocklehurst Grove really is on the hit list."

"We've heard nothing," said Sir Magnus, unconvinced.

"It is still in the early stages," said Albert, "but you will be hearing in the very near future. They're sure to be writing to you."

"What shall we do? We can't live anywhere else but here. You aren't just making this up, are you?" said the old man. Albert's earnest, frightened voice had nothing of the matter-of-fact in it. It might be a matter of fact that information about the road plans was on its way to them, but Albert's voice filled Magnus with the fear of bulldozers and homelessness and being found out.

"It's true enough, I'm afraid. I don't know yet what we should do," said Albert, "but I do think that now is the time we should meet. If it's all right with you, I'll come down Sunday after next. I'll be on holiday then and if necessary, and if you want me, I'll be able to stay for a while."

Sir Magnus felt cornered. He knew that no one in the house really wanted this young man to visit them, however well-meaning he might be. Yet, if the house were really under threat, they would need help. They would need all the help they could get. There was no getting away from that.

"You'd better come, I suppose," he said wearily. "A week on Sunday? Gives us time to get used to the idea."

"I'm not all that bad," said Albert, "and Kate did ask me to help. I'm really not trying to push myself where I'm not wanted."

Sir Magnus suddenly felt ashamed of his ungraciousness.

"It's not that, Albert," he said quite gently. "Don't forget what we are. It'll be a shock to you to see us face to face, and that could be humiliating. We are used to human faces. We see them on television. Those of us who go out see them in the street. We will be the strange ones, and we will feel ashamed of our strangeness."

Now it was said, Sir Magnus felt much better. Till it was said, he did not really know what he meant.

"I know," said Albert. "I understand." Inept he might be in all things practical, but he possessed intelligence and delicacy on a different level. His belief in Kate's people was like a circle that had at that moment become complete. It filled him with pity.

"If we accept how strange we will appear to one another," he said, "I feel sure the strangeness will soon pass."

Aunt Kate's choice of champion was not so very bad after all; an understanding heart is sometimes better than a cool, clear head.

"You will come then," said Sir Magnus, "and you will help."

"If I can do anything, I will," said Albert, sounding

worried. "We'll work out something, all of us together. See you a week Sunday, then."

"A week Sunday," mumbled Sir Magnus and he replaced the receiver without even saying goodbye.

10

Waiting for Albert

The only member of the household wearing spectacles on the following Sunday was Tulip. She had on the usual little glasses that she used for knitting and reading. That was because she had been born wearing them.

It was deemed necessary to miss out the ritual of Sunday lunch.

"We will not make any effort to hide what we are," Soobie had insisted. In fact, Soobie had virtually taken over the conference in Granpa's room.

"We will not have any pretends when Albert Pond is here, if he comes. If there really is a flesh-and-blood Albert Pond who knows all about us, we don't want him to think that we are completely daft. No pretend eating or drinking or anything else. Let him take us as we really are. Any other way is undignified."

Appleby looked at Soobie suspiciously.

"What do you mean 'if' this, 'if' that? Surely you know by now that Albert is real."

The blue-faced Mennym looked straight at her.

"If this is all a hoax," he said, "I don't know how the

52

hoaxer has managed it. But till the real Albert Pond comes in through our front door, we won't be completely sure."

"If he does come," said Vinetta, "I think we should make him welcome. I'll buy some real cake and make some real sandwiches. We'll even give him a real cup of tea."

Appleby looked enchanted.

"It will be just like a pretend," she said, "but it will be real. It's marvellous. I've never thought of anything like that before."

So in the kitchen the kettle was really ready to boil, the tea was in the pot. A willow-patterned cup and saucer stood on the tray together with salmon sandwiches, slices of Madeira cake and some half-chocolate biscuits.

"Where shall we have it?" Vinetta asked.

"Have it?" queried Tulip.

"Where shall we give him his tea?" repeated Vinetta more explicitly.

"On the dining-table of course. Where else?"

"But when Miss Quigley used to be a visitor, we always took her into the lounge," put in Wimpey. "I remember. We always did."

Miss Quigley nodded.

"Albert is different," said Tulip. "He is not family. I think he'll expect to eat at the dining-table. We needn't put the cloth on. I'll just put a place mat at the top of the table and he can sit there."

Miss Quigley said nothing but she glowed warmly at Tulip's implication that she, the visitor, now the nanny, had been given family status.

"And what will *we* be doing whilst Albert eats?" asked Soobie.

"We'll sit round the table and talk to him and keep him

company, of course," said Granny Tulip, looking sternly at Soobie over the top of her little spectacles.

"Won't he wonder why we aren't eating?" asked Pilbeam, feeling a bit uncomfortable about this plan. She couldn't pinpoint why, but it seemed odd.

Soobie gave her question some thought and came up with a logical answer.

"It would be worse if we pretended to eat in front of him. By giving him food, we are accepting him as he is. By not pretending to eat, we avoid looking foolish in his eyes."

Pilbeam still felt uneasy, but she supposed that if Soobie was satisfied, it would be all right.

So there they all were, waiting for the arrival of the visitor. The day-nursery room and the lounge both had a view of the front path. Soobie was in his usual seat by the window. The rest of the family went from one room to the other as the fancy took them. Tulip, of course, just got on with her work. Granpa, naturally, was still in his bed. In due course, Albert would be presented to him and a family conference would be held. It was the younger members of the family who were most excited. Poopie and Wimpey had their faces pressed against the window panes despite repeated attempts by their mother and the rest of the family to get them to behave with more decorum.

Vinetta and Miss Quigley kept checking the tray standing ready in the kitchen.

"It looks all right, doesn't it, Hortensia?" Vinetta asked anxiously.

"It looks lovely," Hortensia reassured her employer. "I could just eat those sandwiches myself, if I could eat," she added with the strange, uncharacteristic grin that sometimes stole across her plain cloth face.

Joshua sat staring gloomily at the gas fire in the lounge.

One of his father's pearls of wisdom kept drifting through his mind — the one about the devil and the deep blue sea.

Then . . .

Albert came.

He really came.

He walked hesitantly up the garden path and they had their first view of him. He was slim and narrow-shouldered. A lock of brown hair flopped over his broad brow. He was eyeing the front of the house as if he thought that something in there was about to come out and eat him. His expression was, if anything, even more bewildered than in his photograph. Vinetta's heart went out to him. He seemed so vulnerable, standing there in a padded jacket that looked too big, his right hand gripping a shabby-looking grey suitcase.

Tulip came out of the breakfast-room when she heard the stir. It was she who opened the door as soon as the bell rang. A poor specimen, she thought, as she looked at the young man on the doorstep, not one to inspire confidence.

"You must be Albert Pond," she said. "Come in. They're all waiting for you."

11

First Encounter

As soon as the doorbell rang, Joshua and Soobie hurried into the dining-room and took their places at the table. The younger twins followed but stayed in the doorway. Appleby and Pilbeam, eaten up with curiosity, stood in the most shadowy part of the hall where the little cloakroom jutted out. Miss Quigley was coming out of the nursery, and Vinetta was just behind Tulip.

So what was the first thing Albert saw as he stepped out of the little lobby into the dimly lit hall? He saw the big square buckles on Miss Quigley's shoes! He dared not look up. He hardly dared to look ahead. So he looked down to his right and there were the buckles, comfortingly real on a very normal pair of ladies' shoes. Tulip's checked apron . . . Vinetta's hands . . . two little heads looking round a doorway – one with a straight fringe across the brow, one with bunches of curls tied up in ribbons. Two older girls in the corner, fidgeting a bit nervously. That was a help. They were nervous too.

"Hello," said Albert.

"Hello," said various voices.

"Into the dining-room, girls," said Vinetta as she took

Albert's coat and put it in the cloakroom. Then she left Tulip to see them all to their places whilst she fetched the tray from the kitchen.

Albert sat at one end of the long, dark, richly polished dining-table. On a very large green mat of loosely woven material, Vinetta placed the plates of food, a cup and saucer, a small matching teapot, a jug of milk and a basin full of sugar lumps. There was even a silver spoon, a tea-knife on a willow-patterned plate, and a delicate pair of sugar tongs. It looked completely right. Vinetta felt proud of herself, especially as she poured the tea and watched the hot brown liquid cascade into the cup.

"I'll let you help yourself to milk and sugar," she said as if she were used to entertaining. "Do have a sandwich. They are all real. I made them myself this morning."

Albert was dazed. The oddness of meeting these people who were genuinely different from the human race, and not just a variation on size, shape or colour, would not sink in. Soobie, acutely aware of being the blue Mennym, had chosen to sit in the shadows on his father's left. To Joshua's right sat Miss Quigley and between Miss Quigley and Vinetta the younger twins shuffled and stared. Albert had Vinetta on his left-hand side and Tulip on his right. Appleby and Pilbeam sat between their grandmother and their silent, cautious brother.

Albert smiled at them all nervously. He stirred his tea and lifted it up to his lips to sip. Nine pairs of eyes watched the cup go up and then down again. Albert looked along the table and his eyes met Joshua's. The distance was just about enough for his host to look fairly human.

Albert picked up a neat, triangular salmon sandwich. Nine pairs of eyes watched in fascination as it disappeared into his mouth. No one said a word. He lifted his cup again and when he put it down the clatter it made as it met the saucer was the loudest noise in the room.

Albert looked round at them all. Nine pairs of beady eyes stared from cloth faces. Albert found himself focussing on the weave of the cloth, and the perfect stitching of each still pair of lips. The Mennyms were so bewitched by this close-up view of a human being that their dollness was taking them over. The glass eyes glittered.

And the spell . . .

The spell was only broken when the terrified young man at the head of the table fell in a faint to the floor.

"Come on, Albert. Wake up. Nobody's going to hurt you!" Tulip bent over him and, for the very first time, touched flesh as her hand moved his face from side to side.

The innocent brown eyes opened wide and Albert looked up into Tulip's crystal gaze. It was as Appleby had foretold (how long ago it seemed!) when she had had them all convinced of the impending visit of the Australian. One look into those crystals that were Tulip's eyes and Albert was more than half hypnotised. We are people, the eyes said, we are living, we are real. We will accept you. You must accept us. Her strong will supplied him with a set of rules, a modus vivendi essential to both sides.

And it worked. Albert would never fear the Mennyms again. He would not even notice that they were anything other than human. He would still know it with the conscious part of his mind, because the knowledge was necessary to their survival. But the subconscious part would accept the Mennyms as ordinary people, which in essence, of course, they were.

"How do you make food disappear, Mr Pond?" Wimpey asked.

"It's easy," said Albert. "Like magic!" He was back on his seat and eating a chocolate digestive biscuit. He smiled at Wimpey and held up the biscuit to show that a segment had really gone. That was how it worked and would always work from then on. The differences between man and doll were openly acknowledged, and dismissed as unimportant.

12

The First Salvo

Letters were delivered to every household in the Grove the day after Albert Pond's arrival. The spring of the letterbox rang out sharply in the silent hall. The thick, official envelope landed heavily in the lobby.

Albert was just waking up from a sound sleep in Soobie's room. The blue Mennym had offered the room on the first floor. It had, after all, been the guest room before Miss Quigley moved in. Soobie had given his old room on the second floor to Miss Quigley so that she need not be on the same landing as Poopie and Wimpey.

"I'll lie on the settee in the lounge," he had insisted when the question of where Albert should sleep had been broached.

"It doesn't seem fair that you should be the one to move again," Vinetta had protested, but not too strongly. If Soobie did not move, it would be much more trying to move any of the others.

"It's taking advantage of good nature," she had said weakly.

"Yes," Soobie replied with a rare smile, "it is! But I

60

honestly don't mind. It'll save me another flight of stairs anyway!" And that was that.

The letter with the Castledean Council's insignia printed on the back, an ominous-looking green portcullis, was picked up by Vinetta, always the earliest to rise. She felt a bit weary that Monday morning. The day before had been stressful. They had all ultimately found it necessary to go back to their pretends.

Joshua was the first to slip up. He quite unconsciously took out his pipe and pretended to light it and draw on it and coax it along in a very realistic manner.

Albert watched him.

Tulip pursed her lips and tried to signal to Joshua.

Soobie looked on, thought about it, and then made up his mind. After all, Albert was no longer a stranger. He had his odd ways too. He was the first person in over forty years to use the lavatory. The sound of the cistern had been startling.

"We pretend things," Soobie explained abruptly. "We are learning to accept you as you are. You are learning to accept us as we are. That is another bit of it. We have our pretends, at least some of us do."

Joshua, totally oblivious, went on contentedly smoking the unlit pipe.

"A pretend pipe is better than the other sort," Albert said with a smile. "It won't do anybody any harm."

In some ways Albert's visit had been fun. The dishes had been genuinely dirty. It had really been necessary to don washing-up gloves to rinse out the tea things. Albert, being a polite young man, had not liked to mention being hungry at suppertime. It was only in the middle of the night that Vinetta had woken up with a start, her subconscious suddenly realising that the visitor would have to be fed all day and every day. It was a worry!

And now the letter! It was just too much. It was addressed to Joshua. Sir Magnus, in his determination to bamboozle the bureaucrats, had removed himself from the electoral register many years before. Vinetta, as usual, did not bother waiting for her husband to come in from work but tore open the envelope immediately and first skimmed, then scanned, its contents.

They were unspecific as to dates and held out vague offers of compensation and a fingers-crossed series of circumlocutions that meant, when it came down to it, compulsory purchase of property to be demolished.

"Oh dear," Vinetta sighed. "Oh dear!"

Albert Pond came down the stairs just at that moment. He had on a white sweatshirt asking people to save the whale, and a pair of dark-coloured jeans. The moment she saw him, looking so casual and comfortably at home, Vinetta panicked.

"We've run out of cornflakes," she said desperately. True, there were no cornflakes, but to say they had run out of them implied that they had once had some, which was just not true at all.

"That's all right," said Albert. "I'll just have some toast, if you don't mind. I never eat much for breakfast."

That was better. There was still half a loaf left from yesterday.

"The toaster's on the shelf in the kitchen. Help yourself to as much as you like."

Vinetta had never used the toaster. It had stood idle for over forty years. She followed Albert into the kitchen and as she filled the kettle to make the tea she watched warily out of the corner of her eye as Albert pushed the plug into the socket and placed two slices of bread in the slots.

"We've had a letter," Vinetta said as they stood waiting for the kettle to boil and the toast to pop, "the one you warned us about."

She handed it over to him and he began to read it, stopped to butter his toast, sat down at the kitchen table, and finished reading as he ate. Two more slices of toast were in the toaster. He suddenly realised that he was hungry after all.

"You must be hungry," said Vinetta, approaching the problem as delicately as she could. "I'm a bit worried about that, Albert. If you are to stay with us for any length of time, you will either have to eat out, or show me how to cook your meals. Pretend cooking is not the same," she finished feebly.

"That's no problem," said Albert looking up from the letter. "I'm used to cooking for myself. I'll get some groceries in today. Have you a freezer?"

"No," said Vinetta, "but there is a very large pantry and it is always quite cold."

"No fridge?" queried Albert. When it came to cooking he was definitely a fridge and freezer man!

"Yes!" said Vinetta, happy to remember the white chest under the bench in the corner. "Of course! What am I thinking of? There is a refrigerator with a little freezer compartment. We defrosted it years ago and left it turned off. Tulip said it was a waste running it for nothing. I'll clean it out today and switch it on again."

Albert returned to the letter.

Vinetta watched him anxiously, hoping that he would understand the parts she had found difficult, but, above all, hoping that this clever young man would spot some life-saving loophole.

"It's obviously in the very early stages," said Albert, when he reached the end of the third page. "There'll be months, if not years, to go before anything really happens."

"But some day something will," said Vinetta.

"Yes," said Albert, "I'm afraid so. Still, it does give us time to prepare."

13

The Purple Foot

The letter was given to Sir Magnus. He had just the faintest twinge of the gout again and, for that reason, among a devious variety of others, he decided that the family should hold a conference on Tuesday. They could all have the rest of Monday to think about it.

Albert had been taken to be presented to the head of the family the previous evening. It had been a brief and not altogether happy encounter. Albert, the scholar, junior lecturer at the university, had not read a single one of Sir Magnus Mennym's articles, not even his account of the Battle of Edgehill.

"There's such a lot to read," Albert had said apologetically. "It's very hard to keep up with it all. I'm not brilliant or anything, just interested. My area of study really ends at 1485 with the Battle of Bosworth Field. The Civil War is too modern, if you see what I mean."

Small beer, thought Sir Magnus, very small beer.

To make it worse, Albert became fascinated by the purple foot that was clearly cloth and not at all realistic. When it was still, it looked foolish. When it moved, it looked unnatural and frightening. Albert tried looking everywhere else in the room, the curtains, the lampshade, the old man's mittened hands, his healthy face with its white walrus moustache; but the eyes were drawn back again and again to the purple foot.

"Does it bother you?" Sir Magnus said at last in an ominous growl.

"What?" Albert asked, blushing.

"My foot, lad. You don't seem to be able to keep your eyes off it. Have you never seen a foot before?"

"Not a purple one," Albert replied, and then wished he hadn't said that.

Tulip came in as they were speaking. She covered her husband's foot with the counterpane. Fixing her crystal gaze on Albert she said, "I think we've all had enough excitement for one day. You'd best be off to bed, Albert. I'll show you your room."

Monday was much better. Poopie and Wimpey tried to persuade Albert to play Monopoly with them. When Vinetta rescued him from that close encounter of the board-game kind, he settled down in the lounge and talked happily to Soobie. It didn't matter at all that Soobie was blue. By the time they had talked for ten minutes, Soobie was just Soobie, Albert was just Albert, and they were well on their way to being friends for life.

Pilbeam and Appleby came down just after mid-day and offered to go with Albert to the supermarket. Vinetta guiltily remembered the vexed question of food.

"Of course," she said. "You must be starving, Albert. Here, Pilbeam, take twenty pounds and buy some groceries. Albert will tell you what to get."

Albert looked uncomfortable.

"Honestly, Vinetta," he said hastily, "I'll see to it myself. Put your money away. I don't want to impose on you."

"Nonsense," said Tulip. "Take the money, Pilbeam. Do the shopping. Albert is our guest. We don't allow guests to pay for their own food."

Albert looked helplessly at Vinetta.

"That's right," said Vinetta. "Do as she says. And stop worrying!"

On the way out Albert, Pilbeam and Appleby passed Miss Quigley coming in with Googles in her pram. It would be hard to say who fluttered the most as they greeted each other – Albert or Hortensia.

As they strode out along the pavement, one either side of Albert, Pilbeam and Appleby both felt very proud. Pilbeam was thinking how nice it was to have another friend, a new member of the family – Nuovo Alberto! Goodness knows what Appleby was thinking! Her thoughts were complicated, exciting and, naturally, selfish. She hung onto Albert's left arm and chattered.

"You could have pretends just like us," she said. "I know Soobie thinks we should try not to have so many pretends when you are here, but never mind him. He's always a spoil sport."

Albert smiled nervously, as well he might.

"You could pretend to be a doctor," Appleby went on, "and come to cure Granpa's gout."

"I don't think so somehow!" said Albert, wincing at the thought of Sir Magnus's purple foot.

"Or you could pretend to be Pilbeam's boyfriend."

Pilbeam was irritated and embarrassed, but she managed to say lightly, "Don't be silly. Albert probably already has a girlfriend. Your pretends get more foolish every day."

Albert too felt embarrassed and taken on the raw.

"I did have a girlfriend," he said. "We were going to be married. Then she went off and married somebody else.

That's why I went abroad. I spent all my savings on that holiday."

Appleby let go of his arm and stood, startled, in front of him. Behind the butterfly sunglasses, her green eyes glowed.

"That's what I told them all," she said. "It's exactly what I said you'd done. I *am* psychic!"

Pilbeam recovered her composure and said with a giggle, "Come off it, Appleby. It was a good guess. That's all."

"Well, you think what you like and I will think what I like," said Appleby, every inch the fiery redhead. And Pilbeam, the dark lady, smiled at her indulgently. Their difference in age might be only one year but sometimes the gap in maturity was much greater.

"You could pretend to be our solicitor and come and make Granpa's will. He would love that. I bet he would leave more to me than to anybody else," said Appleby as they walked on.

"Shut up, Appleby!" said Pilbeam and Albert together, and there and then Albert felt like one of the family.

After the shopping they went home laden with groceries. It was a struggle to fit the frozen food into the tiny freezer compartment of the fridge, especially the chips.

"I'd better use some chips straightaway," said Albert. "There's not really enough room for all of them."

Pilbeam and Appleby watched fascinated as Albert, the culinary expert, cooked himself a meal of beefburgers, baked beans and french fries. The gas cooker had to be lit with a match, being so old, but it still worked perfectly well. Albert sat and ate in the kitchen whilst the girls washed the pans and talked to him.

"Can you drive a car?" asked Appleby. She was thinking of all the ways they might be able to use his greater ability to get around the world.

"Yes," said Albert, "but I haven't got one. My last one packed up and I can't afford a new one yet."

He went on eating and thought regretfully that he should have bought a car instead of spending everything on the holiday.

"If you hadn't spent all your savings on that holiday, you could have bought a car," said Appleby tactlessly.

"That's downright rude," said Pilbeam. "What Albert does or doesn't do is his own business."

Pilbeam found herself remembering Albert's first letter and the mention in it of Comus House. How could he be so out of funds when he had a house he could sell? If he sold it, he should easily be able to afford a car. And if the Mennyms really did need a second home, Grandpa should buy it from him. That would be no more than fair.

14

The Family Conference

Tulip carefully draped the counterpane over Magnus's foot.

"What are you doing that for?" he asked peevishly. "It's irritating."

He pushed the foot out and tugged the counterpane away from it so that it was even possible to see the seam where it was attached to the white cloth that covered his leg.

Tulip gave him a look of severe determination. She pulled the cover over his foot again and said, "Leave it there. Your face is fine, your moustache is most distinguished, your mind is a mass of information, but your feet are definitely Kate's early work. Albert can get used to everything else, but that foot sticking over the edge of the bed disconcerts him. You know it does."

Sir Magnus gave her a look of offended superiority and uttered the pearl of wisdom that maintained that beauty was in the eye of the beholder.

"Sometimes," said Tulip. "But you must keep that foot covered for the conference, and let's have no more argument about it!"

In the next ten minutes they all trooped in and took their places. Albert and Soobie were the last to arrive.

Sir Magnus raised himself high on his pillows, cleared his throat most convincingly and addressed the room.

"This, as you all know, is a most solemn and serious occasion. All manner of things will be happening in the future and we must be prepared. Make no mistake about it, a house, even a house as old and venerable and well-built as this one, can be reduced to rubble. Albert Pond has been sent here to help us in this dire situation. So let us hear first what he has to say."

He looked at Albert very sternly and said, "The floor is yours. You may speak."

It was Albert's turn to clear his throat, a real clearing of a real throat that felt completely choked. His dazed brown eyes, soulful as a spaniel's, went from one to another. All of them, even the younger twins, were sitting tensely waiting. There was no fainting away this time – Tulip's mesmeric crystal gaze saw to that.

"Sir Magnus, Lady Tulip, family," Albert began, trying briefly to match his host's formality, "we've all read this letter that came yesterday morning. Every household in the street will have received one. I've no doubt we'll be hearing from the neighbours. Whenever anything like this happens people tend to get together to see what they can do to stop it."

"We never have anything to do with the neighbours," said Vinetta. "It's impossible. You must know it is, Albert."

"That at least is where I can help. For as long as I am here, I will answer the door. I will talk to the neighbours. I will tell them that we feel that resistance would achieve nothing and that we are moving immediately to our house in the country."

His hearers had very mixed feelings.

"Are we really?" asked Wimpey, her eyes filled with wonder.

Albert looked down at her and smiled.

"That's the next bit," he said. "If you want to, there is a house in the country – the one I mentioned in my first letter to you. It has been in the Penshaw family for generations. It is mine now, and you are all welcome to stay there."

"You were going to sell it," put in Soobie, trying to protect his new friend from foolish generosity. It was one of the many things they had talked about the day before. "You're not rich enough to give it away."

Albert looked uncomfortable.

"It doesn't matter," he said. "Nobody wants to buy it anyway. And it is the family's house. Kate wants you to have it."

"Ghosts can't own property," argued Soobie, "but rag dolls can. We own this house, don't we? If we take over your house, we should pay for it."

It was true. They did own the house. It had been left to them by Chesney Loftus, Aunt Kate's real nephew who really had lived, and died, in Australia. He had thought they were real tenants, staying on in the house after his aunt's death. They had paid him rent for the past forty-odd years, perfect tenants, punctual in their payments and never asking for any repairs to be done. Chesney's bequest had been an acknowledgement of this. There was a codicil, but not one likely to trouble them. It just meant that every year, on the first of October, either Sir Magnus or Joshua had to sign an assertion that they were still in residence. This document had to be sent special delivery to their own solicitor who would pass it on to Cromarty, Varley and Thynne, the solicitors for the estate of the deceased.

Sir Magnus nodded agreement with Soobie's proposal that they should consider buying a second home.

Lady Tulip, however, looked businesslike and doubtful.

"If no one else is rushing to buy it, perhaps we should take our time before making any rash decisions. It may not be suitable for us. We would certainly have to look at it first. That's the very least we should do."

"Look before we leap," said Magnus, deciding that, after all, discretion might be the better part of valour. Tulip, he knew, was no fool when it came to business transactions. The words about being wary of buying a pig in a poke drifted into his mind, but he had just enough tact not to use them!

"He who hesitates is lost," said Appleby.

"A stitch in time saves nine," said Poopie, recognising the game.

"Stop it, all of you," said Vinetta. "This is much too serious for silly jokes. We need as many details as you can give us, Albert. Tell us where this house is, whether it is big enough for all of us, and how soon we would have to move. The rest of you sit still and listen."

"Comus House," said Albert, "is bigger than this one, but it is a bit older and it hasn't had much done to it for the last sixty years or so. It was one of the first houses in the area to be lit by electricity, but after that time stood still. My grandparents both lived in the past. They seemed to think it would have been better if the twentieth century had never happened. No one has really lived there since my grandfather died. It was left to my father, but my mother refused to live in it. Still, it is quite strongly built. If you decided to settle there and could put a few thousand into renovating it, I think you would find it homely enough."

There was a united, instinctive opposition to the idea of moving. The complications were terrifying.

"I have my job to think about," said Joshua. "I don't want to move away from here."

"Nobody does," said Vinetta, "but it looks as if we may not have much choice."

"How long can you stay with us, Albert?" asked Appleby. Pilbeam looked sharply at her sister. She knew how inventive Appleby could be and Appleby definitely had an inventive expression on her face.

"I suppose I could stretch to three weeks," said Albert, "but I'll have to be back for the start of term."

"Right," said Appleby. "This is what we do. You, Albert, will go to the neighbours with a petition which we will all sign. You can sign too, Albert, as an interested party. You'll tell everybody how upset we are, but that we don't want to talk about it. You can say something like, 'They're a funny family, distant cousins of mine. They don't mix with strangers – eccentric, but harmless you know. All this is hitting them very hard.' That should work, I think."

"Then what?"

"Then you'll have started the ball rolling. They'll take over the petition and they won't bother us. We'll just be the cranky lot that live at Number 5."

"The best form of defence is attack," commented Sir Magnus.

Albert was impressed with Appleby's reasoning, but then he started to think ahead.

"What if the petition fails? It probably will fail. Then what?"

"We'll have bought time," said Appleby. "At this moment all we need to worry about are nosy neighbours. It will be ages and ages before the council officials get any further. Before then we can try Comus House to see if it will do."

"Thank you," said Albert wryly.

"I don't mean it like that," said Appleby. "What I mean is that when your summer vacation comes, we can hire a minibus and you can take us there. Father's annual holiday is the last week in June and the first in July. How about it?"

Sir Magnus gave his granddaughter a look of admiration.

"How on earth do you know about hiring – what was it you said? – a minibus?"

"I know loads of things, Granpa. What I wasn't born knowing, I make it my business to find out."

Pilbeam said doubtfully, "I don't see what good it would do to spend a holiday at Comus House if we are not going to settle there. It might be fun for us, but it would be a dreadful upheaval for Granny and Granpa. They are old, you know."

Appleby knew this already, but she also knew that there was far more chance of persuading her father to go away for two weeks than there was of getting him to hand in his notice at Sydenham's. Once they got him there, it might be just possible to persuade him to stay.

Tulip and Magnus were so offended at being called old that they remained silent.

"We must go," said Appleby, wishing she were sitting near enough to give Pilbeam a sly dig. "Once people start making a fuss about preserving Brocklehurst Grove, this place will be in the spotlight. There will be protesters and reporters all over the place. Not to mention council officials. We can't risk living in this house if the street becomes the focus of attention. We go away. If the petition succeeds, we sneak quietly back. If it fails, we settle elsewhere."

Joshua looked at her suspiciously. There was double-talk

in there somewhere. A two-week holiday, whilst things were being sorted out, was one thing. An extended stay in the country was out of the question. Joshua remained silent, but he thought the more.

Vinetta watched him and knew what he was thinking.

"We may not need to stay long," she said. "The petition sounds a good idea. Our own house might be saved."

"It should be," said Miss Quigley. "It might not be as old as Comus House, but it has been standing for over a hundred years. This street has character. It should be protected."

Joshua had been quietly considering all they said.

"It strikes me," he said, "that all we need concern ourselves with for now is the petition. We'll just take the rest as it comes."

That was the final word. They filed out of the room leaving Tulip to straighten the chairs and put them back where they belonged. Granpa's foot slid comfortably out of its cover.

"Glad that's over," he said, but his black button eyes looked glazed and his fine white moustache drooped. He was losing heart, even with conferences. His pearls of wisdom now seemed like pygmies in a land of giants.

Tulip too felt despondent.

"Life used not to be like this," she said. "Once it was quiet and humdrum. Now it is just one crisis after another. Maybe Appleby sowed the wind when she invented the Australian. Now we are reaping the whirlwind."

"A pearl of wisdom," said her husband with a sad smile, "a terrifying pearl of wisdom."

15

The Move

Albert stayed three weeks and, considering his natural lack of confidence, he put on a magnificent performance. He went to see all of the neighbours. He wrote to the local newspaper protesting against the vandalism of knocking down the statue of Matthew James Brocklehurst and the terrible shame of demolishing a street of such gracious, well-proportioned houses. Research had given him the information that the said Matthew James had been a leader in the Methodist Movement, a great supporter of Sunday Schools and Workers' Institutes. It was promising material.

It was only after Albert had made the acquaintance of the family at Number 9 that he felt able to pass the baton. The Fryers were wonderful. If anyone could save Brocklehurst Grove, they were the ones to do it.

Loretta Fryer was a concert pianist. Her husband, Alexander, was a television producer. Their only daughter, Anthea, owned and ran a small picture gallery.

"I'm sorry, Albert," she said with a shake of her head, "you just won't do. It will take real salesmanship to put over the idea of saving the Grove. I don't wish to be unkind, but you're not the type to argue with That Lot. You'd have to be a sight more brash."

Albert smiled at her. He might not be brash, but he did have a sense of humour. Anthea, standing there with her firm chin and vividly blue eyes, looked so self-consciously determined. Her blonde hair was cut in a short, neat bob with a half-fringe that licked her right eyebrow. Her shoulders were broad and she was about four inches taller than Albert.

"You're an Amazon," he said, smiling. "I'll leave the whole protest in your capable hands. I have to be back in Durham in three days' time whatever. I'll try to keep in touch. But do remember to leave the Mennyms in peace. I don't want to be faced with an epidemic of nervous breakdowns in the family. They can't help the way they are."

Anthea was quite pleased to be called an Amazon. It agreed with her own opinion of herself. But she knew how to pity the weak. Number 5, with its bunch of reclusive residents, would be out of bounds to everybody. She regarded them as an endangered species. "If you want to know how things are going," she said, "just pop in some time or ring me at work." Albert's first objective was safely achieved.

When Albert returned at the end of June with the minibus, evidence of Anthea's determination greeted him as he drove down the main road. There, on a banner nine foot deep, strung from the roof of Number 1 right across the front of the Grove to the roof of Number 9, were the words

SAVE BROCKLEHURST GROVE!

The letters were brilliant red on a white background.

"Did you see the banner?" asked Wimpey excitedly before Albert had even crossed the doorstep.

"It would be hard to miss it," said Albert. "The Amazon doesn't do things by halves!"

"Are we going in that bus?" asked Poopie, wide-eyed. "When can we go? Can we have a ride in it now?"

Vinetta chased Poopie and Wimpey off to the playroom.

"Come into the lounge, Albert," she said, "and sit down. I'll make you a nice cup of tea and some sandwiches. Then, when you're ready, we'll go up and see Magnus."

The hardest bit would be getting Sir Magnus unobtrusively on to the bus. Albert had managed, with only inches to spare, to park it in the drive. But a minibus, even in this very private street, was liable to arouse curiosity.

"I shall have to get dressed, I suppose," said Magnus with no great enthusiasm.

Tulip looked doubtful, wondering what her husband was going to wear.

Albert was more concerned about the old man's ability to walk down two flights of stairs and out into the drive. A chair lift? He and Soobie might be able to do it, but he wasn't at all sure.

"How will you manage the stairs?" he asked tentatively.

The white moustache quivered, the black beady eyes bulged.

"How do you think I'll manage them?" he said. "Like anybody else of course. What do you think I am?"

Albert felt flustered, but he found himself looking almost spitefully at the purple foot that Sir Magnus's rage had uncovered again. It certainly did not look serviceable for walking on.

Sir Magnus dismissed them from his room for twenty minutes. When they were allowed to return, the sight amazed them. Sir Magnus was standing centre stage as it were, dressed in a Norfolk jacket, plusfours and a deerstalker hat.

The purple feet were hidden in diamond-patterned socks and crammed into a huge pair of country brogues.

"Well?" he said, raising his white bushy eyebrows.

Albert did not know what to say.

Tulip did.

She smiled at her husband sweetly and said, "Perfect, Magnus. Quite perfect."

Her mind did rapid, anxious calculations. If they left in mid-afternoon the street should be quiet. There should be no one around to notice. Dusk would have been better, but dusk comes too late in June.

"When do we have to leave?" asked Joshua. "It can't be before Friday. Remember I'm at work on Thursday night."

"We'll leave on Friday afternoon at two-thirty," said his mother with precision.

The bus journey was brilliant. The things the Mennyms were born knowing included many a bus-trip, of course. But this! This was a happening-now thing, a heightened reality.

They sang. Appleby led the singing, putting her own words to a tune she remembered from her days in the Brownies. (It was part of her built-in memory that she had once been a Brownie. It was only half a memory, dimly related to the children's books she had, or maybe had not, read.)

> "Here we go like sparrows in the wilderness,
> Sparrows in the wilderness
> Sparrows in the wilderness.
> Here we go like sparrows in the wilderness,
> Looking for a place to hide.
> Looking for a place to
> Looking for a place to

Looking for a place to
HIDE!"

Albert, in the driving seat, smiled at the words, recognising Appleby's acuteness of perception in their sentiments. Soobie, in the corner of the back seat, scowled at the back of Appleby's head. Pilbeam joined in the singing, and swayed to the rhythm, but kept her voice well-modulated. Poopie and Wimpey became very excited and sang loudly and tunelessly, belting out the last word vigorously, then starting all over again.

Googles began to grizzle. Not even the best baby ever invented could sleep through that row. Miss Quigley jiggled the baby on her knee. She looked back over her shoulder and said, "Can't you keep those two a bit quieter, Appleby? They're upsetting Googles. The poor lamb doesn't know what's happening."

Appleby pulled a face, but at the same time she was flattered that Miss Quigley had given her the responsibility for calming down the twins. With a sly look at Pilbeam, she said in a sugary voice, "Yes, Miss Quigley. I'll see to them."

Pilbeam said helpfully, "Tell them a story, Appleby. They always enjoy your stories."

Appleby felt inspired.

"Do you want to know what Comus House is like?" she said.

"You don't know," said Poopie scornfully. "You haven't been there either."

"Not in this life," said Appleby, looking solemn, "but I have been on this earth before. I have lived other lives."

Soobie groaned.

The twins looked at their sister wide-eyed. Even the grown-ups began to listen. Only Sir Magnus, asleep in the left-hand side front seat, and Albert, busy with his driving, took no notice.

"In a previous existence," went on Appleby, "I was a lady, a proper lady, married to a lord, not just a knight's wife."

Tulip was offended but said nothing.

"I lived in the manor that is now called Comus House. I can see it now, built of rugged stone with turrets at each corner. And inside there is the great hall, the wide, sweeping staircase, corridors with family portraits on their walls, a music gallery above the refectory, and bedroom after bedroom after bedroom. It was built in the time of James the First. Some parts of it are even older."

She paused and slumped forward with a deep, musical sigh as if the effort had been too great.

"What else, Appleby?" asked Poopie, eagerly shaking her arm.

Appleby looked up, startled.

"There's a well in the courtyard where a child once drowned."

"That's horrible," said Wimpey. "You're making it all up."

"Stop it, Appleby," said Pilbeam sharply. "It's not fair to frighten them."

At first the bus was travelling along a winding road through green and yellow fields. Tracks led up to isolated farmhouses and their outbuildings. There were no villages along this road. Once they saw a group of houses with a church steeple, miles away on the horizon. Then the fields ceased and the road skirted a steep, rough hillside. Far to the west of them was acre upon acre of brushy moorland.

There were stakes along this roadway. They must have been about ten or twelve foot high and rose from the moorside every few yards.

Poopie watched them for some time. He looked round

the bus and then decided that his father was the most likely to know the answer to the question he just had to ask.

"What are those wooden posts for, Dad? They're set up like street-lamps, but they're just bits of wood."

Joshua looked back at him and said, "They're for when it snows."

It was a brief enough explanation, but it was clear what he meant. They all shuddered as they thought of a coming winter cut off in snow so deep that even the road could be totally lost under it. And Comus House would only be reached by following markers protruding from drifts of snow . . .

As they came to a very wide curve to the right where the narrow road was going uphill quite sharply and whatever was round the bend was masked by hedgerows, Albert called out to them, "We're nearly there. The house is up on your right just after the bend."

The first thing they saw as the bus rounded the corner was a white wooden gate. From it a steep, steep path of about a hundred steps cut into the hillside led up to a distant house.

"There's a marvellous view of the moors from up there," said Albert proudly, "and hills miles and miles away."

Sir Magnus woke with a jolt as the bus stopped in front of the gate. He looked at the steps. The house at the top of them was so far away that it was no more than an outline.

"That is impossible," he said. "Totally and absolutely impossible."

"I just stopped to let you have your first view of it," said Albert hastily. "We don't use the steps. Nobody ever uses the steps."

"Are you thinking of hiring a helicopter?" asked Magnus.

Albert gave a nervous laugh.

"Don't worry, Sir Magnus, there is a much easier way in. A little further on there are some big double gates leading to a cart track that takes us up into the garage. I'll drive right up there and then you have just a very short way to go on a level path to get to the house itself."

"Well, let's get a move on then," said the old man impatiently. "We've seen your view. Now let's get up to the house and stop hanging around for nothing."

16

Comus House

The front of the house was very long and totally flat without a gable or an ingle to relieve the monotony of windows. It was constructed of dull red brick and definitely early Victorian. Ivy grew up the walls, not lushly but in a straggly, weary way. The whole building was sombre and sooty-looking, like a grim prison.

"Wuthering Heights," said Soobie as he looked up at it.

"Bleak House," said Pilbeam.

"Very bleak house," said Appleby with a groan.

"It looks haunted," said Wimpey. And at that moment a large, black bird flapped noisily up from the roof.

"You said it was built of stone and had turrets . . ." began Poopie, looking accusingly at Appleby. He had imagined towers and battlements, a castle almost. This drab, austere building was a real disappointment.

"It was just a story, Poopie," said Appleby. "You all enjoyed it. I can't help it if you are too gullible. Soobie didn't believe me. Neither did Pilbeam."

Miss Quigley, standing with Googles in her arms, looked annoyed and embarrassed. She had believed in the Jacobean house with the family portraits and the music gallery. She felt cheated. So, to a lesser extent, did Tulip and Vinetta.

"Albert never contradicted you," said Vinetta.

"He wasn't listening."

Albert wasn't listening now either. He was standing on the doorstep with the key in his hand. It was a huge key, a regular town-gaol type. The door was stout and deeply studded.

"Come on then," said Sir Magnus, leaning heavily on his cane, "let's get inside."

Albert put the key in the lock.

"I don't come here very often," he said apologetically. "Nearly everything is under dust sheets. It's a bit . . . well, you'll see what I mean soon enough."

The large door creaked open. They entered cautiously. The hall was dark and musty. The door swung shut behind them, and although it was still bright outside and quite warm, there was a winter chill on the inside air and a deep darkness in every corner.

"I don't like it here," said Wimpey quietly. She gripped Pilbeam's hand.

"We could try switching the light on," said Granny Tulip. She glanced at Albert.

"The electricity's on," he said. "All the services are on, even the telephone. I saw to that a week ago."

Soobie, who was nearest, pushed down the switch. Two of the three bulbs in the ceiling lamp were working. The light shone on the oak-panelled hall, dark and heavily varnished. The carpet that ran up the middle of the stairs was held in place by thick brass rods. Everywhere looked dusty.

Albert talked. He talked a bit like a tour guide as they all stood in the centre of the hall looking bewildered.

"The house dates back to the early nineteenth century.

One of my ancestors was a mine owner. No sign of a mine now, no pit wheel, no mine-shafts. The whole area is given over to sheep farming these days. It's a big place. The families were big then and they had servants, some of them living in."

"Elegant," said Appleby.

"Not specially," said Albert. "Labour was very cheap. We were never a really posh family — just a bit better off than others."

As they walked through the rooms on the ground floor, the whole family felt dismayed. Vinetta gazed in silent horror at the huge kitchen with its old fire range and its deep, chipped, discoloured sink. A clothes pulley with thick wooden slats and wrought-iron brackets stretched the length of the ceiling. There was a washing machine. An electric washing machine. But it belonged to the generation before last, or even earlier! A heavy hand-wringer hung down at its side. There was a tap on the front for the emptying of it. In its day it had been a step forward, its motor swirling the clothes around much more efficiently and with much less effort than a hand-held poss-stick. It could claim to be a very good agitator. It was still a good agitator! It certainly agitated Vinetta.

"I couldn't use that," she said, horrified. "I could get seriously wet."

"They would need cheap labour," said Tulip in her usual forthright way, "and lots of it."

She removed a dust sheet from the piano in the lounge. It was an amazing object with bulbous legs and a candle-holder projecting either side of the music stand.

Wimpey found an old coffee-pot on the sideboard. It was a grey jug, rough like the bark of a tree. White boughs and branches twisted around it. Up one side climbed a boy, his brimmed hat lying behind him, obviously making his way towards a bird's nest. The other side of the jug showed the end of the story. The grinning boy was on his way down carrying the hat, full of chicks, in his hand. The mother bird with a worm in her beak was looking for her babies.

"Can I have it?" said Wimpey eagerly, wrapping her mittened hand around the bough that formed the handle.

"Oh, no!" said Albert, leaping to the rescue. "That belonged to my great-great-great-grandmother."

Poopie was lying under the piano, trying to play it from the inside. Albert watched them all anxiously, worried about what would happen next. The legs of the piano were screwed in, he remembered, and one of them was definitely loose!

Joshua looked at him kindly. He knew, oh how well he knew, that his family were a bit overpowering at times.

"We'd best sit down," he said firmly. Dust sheets were removed from armchairs and sofas. They all slumped into them and fell silent.

"This used to be the drawing-room," said Albert, trying to make conversation. "Funny how many names one room can have — lounge, sitting-room, drawing-room, parlour. This one was always called a drawing-room. When I was little I used to wonder who used to draw here."

He was talking on and on to cover the uncomfortable silence. Then even he ran out of words.

Sir Magnus cast his black gaze on everything and everyone in the room.

"What a state of affairs!" he said at last. "Out of the frying pan into the fire!"

Albert looked mortified.

"I'm sorry," he said. "I really am sorry."

"You thought that just because we were rag dolls anything would do for us," said Sir Magnus.

"That's not fair," said Vinetta. "Albert has done his best. He was very good with the neighbours at Brocklehurst Grove. He has gone to the bother of driving us all the way here. If we haven't the gumption to make the place habitable, then we can't blame him. He did warn us that it would need renovation."

"Some of these things will be worth a lot of money," said Tulip, astute as usual. "Whatever changes we make we'll have to be careful not to damage anything of value. And items like that jug should be locked away."

"I could make a go of the gardens," said Joshua. "If Poopie and I spend the next two weeks out there you'll not know it for the same place when we go home."

Tulip looked at him sternly.

"We won't be going home, Josh," she said. "This will have to be home now and we must make the best of it."

Joshua looked stubborn.

"I am going home in time for work at the end of my holidays. You can all stay here whilst the business of the Grove is sorted out. I will live quietly at home in our own house and keep an eye on things."

"How will you get there?" asked Poopie. The minibus had to be returned next day. Albert planned to use public transport, walking a mile and a half to a bus-stop on the moor road. Such an alternative was not open to the Mennyms. They could never travel on an ordinary bus. It would put them in much too close proximity with human beings.

"I'll get there," said Joshua doggedly.

Tulip accepted his decision and knew that a means to get him home would have to be found. It was, after all, not such a bad idea. Someone should watch their old home, no matter what the outcome. Niggling at the back of her mind there was also the matter of the codicil. Chesney's will had left the family what was intended to be only a "life" interest in the house: "For however long Sir Magnus Mennym and/ or his son Joshua Mennym should continue to reside in the said property". After which it would 'devolve' to another branch of the Penshaw family.

"You will be there to sign that form when it comes," said Tulip. "You will be able to confirm in all honesty that you are still in residence."

In the meantime, they should get on with making Comus House a bit more comfortable.

"We won't spend too much money on renovations till we know the worst," said Tulip, "but we can all buckle to and do some cleaning and polishing. It's amazing what a difference soap and water can make!"

Appleby gave the room a look of pity. Once Granny Tulip buckled to, there was no stopping her!

"First," said Tulip, "I'll get a room ready for Granpa. He'll still have his work to do and he needs his rest."

Magnus nodded his approval. Within a very short time he was ensconced in a four-poster bed in the best front bedroom. Under Tulip's guidance, Joshua had removed the dusty drapes ready for washing. An ancient but functioning Hoover was used on the carpets, and its single weighty tool attachment sucked the dirt from chairs and curtains. Tulip supervised and directed. The family worked with a will. Appleby and Pilbeam limited their efforts to their own bed-rooms, but that still gave them plenty to do. Poopie and Wimpey fetched and carried. Joshua and Soobie were the workhorses, moving heavy furniture, reaching high shelves, climbing ladders and generally doing whatever Tulip com-manded. Miss Quigley kept Googles by her till she had made the nursery clean enough. Then she left the baby sleeping in her cot and went to help Vinetta. Vinetta worked harder, faster and longer than any of them. She also accepted as her lot the burden of sorting out squabbles when the same piece of equipment was needed in three rooms simultaneously. There weren't enough buckets and brooms to go round. The solitary Hoover was as precious as gold.

They did not clean every room. Comus House was a very long building, built on three floors with attics above. The attics were little rooms with windows tucked under the eaves. In former times they had been the servants' sleeping quarters. It was a mean house for all its size, very dark with narrow, twisting passages and misshapen rooms. The Mennyms took over the first two floors on the south side. The only exception was the library which Soobie, with his infallible instinct for such things, found along a narrow passage that detoured round two unused rooms before reaching the north corner of the house. As they cleared the rooms they needed to use, the family felt as if they were camping out. It was not the same as occupying a whole house.

It took two days of hard work to make even their chosen part of the house fully habitable.

At the end of the second day, Vinetta collapsed into an armchair and said, "I feel like a wet rag." Then she went off into a fit of giggles that alarmed her teenage daughters so much that they raced to the back of the house to find Joshua.

"It's Mum," said Appleby, "I think it's been too much for her. She's going mad."

By the time they had dragged their father to the drawing room, Vinetta had fallen fast asleep. Joshua gently took the duster from her hand, put a cushion behind her head, and made her comfortable.

17

The Stables

"This used to be a well — years and years ago, long before I was born. They had it covered over because a child once fell in and was drowned."

They were out in the yard at the back of the house — Albert and all the younger members of the family.

It was a huge yard. The well was near the high rough-stone wall that separated the Penshaw property from the land beyond. It still had the appearance of a well, a cylindrical brick stump with a slab of concrete covering the top.

They all looked at it and shuddered.

"That's what you said," said Wimpey, looking at Appleby. "In the bus. Remember. You said about the well and the little girl who drowned."

"It wasn't a girl," said Appleby without any hesitation. "It was a boy."

Albert looked astonished.

"You're right," he said. "It was a boy. How did you know?"

Appleby shivered.

"I don't know," she said. "When I try to be psychic it

never works. But sometimes things come to me out of the blue. I don't like it. Pretends are better."

Pilbeam felt protective towards her sister.

"It's just a coincidence, Appleby," she said. "Don't worry yourself about it. If we make a lot of random guesses, some are bound to be true."

Appleby didn't look convinced.

To one side of the yard was a building that had once been the stables and had also served as a garage in later days.

"Let's look over there," said Soobie. He felt clumsy and uncomfortable and out of place. Sometimes even a sixteen-year-old can feel quite old.

The sky was overcast. The day was sultry.

"I think it's going to rain," said Albert as they walked towards the stable door. Within seconds, heavy drops began to fall.

"It's just a shower," said Albert as they hurried inside. "We'll wait in here till it stops. We'd get soaked if we tried to cross the yard."

The stable had no windows, only shutters which were closed. Some daylight came through the ridges in the wood. Albert went to a shelf where lamps and things were kept. They were safety lamps like miners take with them down the pit. Albert found all he needed to get three of them alight. Then the stable became well enough illuminated for them to look around. No horses, of course. No cars. Up the centre was a wooden plank staircase leading to a hay-loft. Towards the back were the remains of what might have been stalls for the animals. The floor to the rear was made of well-worn stone slabs. At the front it had a covering of concrete.

The only object of any interest was an old motor scooter, a sturdy-looking beast with a double seat, a large storage compartment at the back and a broad panel like a shield at the front. Draped over the handlebars was a heavy, well-padded helmet.

"I'd like a go on that," said Soobie surprisingly. Soobie of the armchair, the melancholy Mennym, was actually showing a flicker of enthusiasm.

"I don't see why not," said Albert. "It's pretty ancient, belonged to my father, but it still works. I had it out last summer."

The rain stopped. Albert checked the vehicle and poured some petrol from a large can into its tank.

"It won't take you far on that," he said, "but a few spins round the yard should be all right."

"That's all I had in mind," said Soobie. How wonderful it would have been to ride away on it, to eat up the miles! But Soobie had had more than forty years of facing up uncompromisingly to his own distressing limitations.

"Put the helmet on," said Albert, without considering whether in his case such protection would be necessary.

Soobie did so, and he ceased to be a blue Mennym, especially when he pulled on the large leather gloves that he had found folded up inside the helmet. The blue-striped suit looked incongruous, as if its wearer had come out in his pyjamas, but Soobie did not know that (and would not have cared anyway). He got on to the seat of the scooter.

"I'll show you how . . ." began Albert, feeling a bit anxious.

"No need," said Soobie. "I can ride it. No problem. All clear everyone. Chocks away!"

With that he rode off round the yard, up to the far wall, circling the well, down past the back of the house and along the gravel path that led to the stable again. As he passed the watchers at the stable door he raised his left hand and waved briefly, then continued for another circuit.

"Can I have a turn?" asked Poopie.

"You'd be too small," said Albert. "It takes a bit of hand-ling. Soobie is quite a solid fellow. He looks as if he were born to it."

Albert by now was totally at ease with the Mennyms. Born to it . . . born knowing . . . born at all . . . were all as one. It wasn't important.

"Wouldn't you like to try, Pilbeam?" Albert asked Soobie's twin with a teasing smile. He knew what the answer would be; the question was asked in fun.

"No, thank you!" said Pilbeam. She was delighted to see her brother enjoying himself, but she felt no inclination to hurtle around the yard as he was doing. It was not her style.

"I'd like to try," said Appleby, "and I am big enough."

"No," said Pilbeam. "I'd rather you didn't, Appleby. I'm sure Granny Tulip is looking out of the window. She'd only be annoyed with you. She's probably longing for Soobie to finish his ride."

Appleby tossed her head so that her red hair, worn long and loose today, shook like a mane.

"I don't care what Granny thinks. If I want to ride on the scooter, I will. I know I could ride it every bit as well as Boy Blue."

Pilbeam gave her sister a very stern look.

"You care what I think," she said in acid tones, "and I think you shouldn't ride that scooter, and I think you shouldn't call Soobie silly names, especially in front of other people."

Appleby looked sulky, but she said no more.

Tulip, watching from the kitchen window, was relieved when Soobie finished his ride and put the scooter away.

18

Using Albert

"Buy a Range Rover," said Sir Magnus, fixing Albert with a glassy stare. "See my wife about the money."

Albert was sitting on a well-cushioned loom chair by the bed. He had been summoned there specially that afternoon. The family had been living in Comus House for a week and a half.

"They're very expensive," said Albert, wondering if Sir Magnus really knew about money. The older man gave him a knowing look.

"We don't use Monopoly money," he said. "We have had forty-odd years of earning, accumulating, and probably judicious speculating if I know Tulip. She is the expert at making money grow. See her."

Tulip had her own office in the house by now. It was the cleanest, neatest and barest room in the house – another 'breakfast-room', next to the kitchen, facing out onto the stableyard. Albert did not tell her that it was one of two rooms that had been kept for his own use on occasional visits.

"Cleaner than the others," she had said, looking round the small room on the first day. "This'll do for me."

Albert had been allowed to keep his own bedroom, another smallish, simple room on the first floor at the end of a long narrow passage.

"That's my bedroom whenever I stay here," he had said without opening the door. A wise move. Tulip might well have fancied it for herself!

"We can't afford a brand new car," she said when Albert told her of Sir Magnus's decision. "Waste of money. Still, we do need a vehicle, out here in the wilds."

She skimmed through a copy of Motoring Weekly which just happened to be on her desk!

"That one," she said, pointing to an advertisement for a five-year-old model, "or something like it."

The price would still have been much too high for Albert, but Tulip was even more intimidating than her husband. She looked at him with that nice, tolerant, sweet-old-lady expression, and he knew. He knew!

"I'll write you a cheque," she said. "Fill in the exact amount when you know what it is. Make sure you get all the right paperwork."

Another thought occurred to Albert.

"Who will drive the car?" he asked.

"That's a stupid question," said Tulip. "You will. Who else?"

Albert's brown eyes shone. All right – it would not be his very own car. But he would be the driver, the only driver.

"What about the tax and insurance?" he asked. "Have you thought about them?"

"I told you to see to the paperwork. What do you think paperwork is? Get the car. Get it on the road. And take Joshua home to Brocklehurst Grove. He is due back at work on Monday."

So that was what it was all about! Well, that among other things.

"I could have hired a car for the day," said Albert, determined to be fair.

"There'll be other times when we'll need a car, Albert. This is the back of beyond. We'll need a car and we'll need you. I can't say I am happy about the situation, but we'll just have to learn to live with it."

Within two days, Albert had the Range Rover bought, taxed, insured and baptised with the fire of being thoroughly inspected inside and out and underneath by Poopie and Wimpey who found it completely enchanting.

Joshua was delighted. On Sunday evening he got into the sturdy, dark green vehicle and heaved a sigh of relief as he fastened his seat belt and settled down in the front passenger seat. Apart from Sir Magnus, everyone was there to see him off, even Miss Quigley with Googles in her arms. Albert climbed up into the driving seat.

"I'll be back next Friday," he said. "There are some things I need to see to in Durham. I'll give you a ring in case there's anything you want."

"Mind how you go," said Vinetta.

"Why can't we come?" complained Poopie.

"Next time," said Albert. "I'll take you for a nice long drive next weekend."

Tulip decided she would have to discuss the question of petrol with that young man, but for the moment she let it pass.

In the weeks that followed Joshua's departure, Tulip was to learn that her reservations about Albert were unnecessary. He was totally honest. He used the car fairly, paid for his own petrol and drove with all due care and attention. He and Tulip were soon getting along famously. He liked to have everything down in black and white. He liked the books to balance. These were traits that endeared him to Lady Mennym! She revised her earlier opinion of him. He might look unimpressive but he had his fair share of good points. He was open and honest. He knew how to get straight to the point. He seemed fairly intelligent, even though his wide brown eyes often looked startled. Tulip came to see him as a likeable innocent, but very manageable and very, very useful.

"Now, Albert," she said one day, "I have something I want you to do for me."

Albert felt like hiding. He liked Tulip, he respected Tulip, but no relationship is perfect. Tulip, he soon discovered, always had something she wanted doing. Not like Vinetta! Poor Vinetta struggled on with the housework, making the place look cleaner and tidier every day. She even put on a mackintosh and wellingtons to do the washing, giving Albert a wan smile when he came into the kitchen.

"That must be hard," he had said guiltily. "Let me put the clothes through the wringer for you."

"No," Vinetta had said firmly. "You do enough for us. I'll be all right. It does feel a bit odd doing the work dressed up like this, but it is better than getting sopping wet."

Tulip had also seen Vinetta hard at work. She did not go so far as to offer to help, but she did have some ideas on the subject. The thing she wanted Albert to do this time was not for her own benefit but for that of her daughter-in-law.

"We need a new washing machine," she said.

Tulip flipped through the pages of a catalogue which just happened to be on her desk! Albert was soon to learn that Tulip always managed to have at her fingertips any information she might need. Her collection of catalogues was prodigious.

"That one," she said.

"It's an automatic. It'll need to be plumbed in," said Albert doubtfully.

"You can see to that," said Tulip. "We'll all stay out of the way till the plumber's gone. It shouldn't take him long."

The plumber from Allenbridge was amazed when he saw the kitchen.

"I haven't seen a kitchen like this since I was a lad. It should be in the Beamish Museum!"

"This was my grandparents' house, Mr Golightly," said Albert, not taking offence. "Even for their time, they lived in the past. I'm going to have it completely modernised eventually, but I need the washing machine straightaway."

The plumbing took two days. There were complications. More parts were needed, pipes to go here, tubes to go there.

"There now," said Mr Golightly when he had finished at last. "At least you've got your washer going." He looked round the room speculatively. "It's not a bad shaped kitchen this, plenty of scope. Soon as you're ready, give me a ring. Don't bother with any of them fancy planners. They'll charge you fancy prices. I'll give you a fair deal and do you a good job."

"I'll think about it," said Albert.

"Has he gone?" asked Wimpey from the stairs after the door banged shut. "Is he not coming back this time?"

"He's gone," said Albert, "gone for good. Come on down all of you and see the washing machine."

Vinetta rang Joshua.

"I have an automatic washing machine," she told him. "It's wonderful, Josh. Much better than the twin tub. Just wait till you see it!"

19

Miss Quigley

Comus House faced west over a wide expanse of moorland stretching to a distant range of overlapping hills. Its grounds were unlike the gardens at Brocklehurst Grove. To the back there was no garden at all, just the huge, cobbled stable-yard with the well near the rear wall. To the north side was the stable, which might at one time have been a barn and in later days had housed a family of cars. From the stable a rutted track, the width of two carriages, sloped down to the roadway. To the far side of this track was a vegetable garden.

The garden in front of the house was split in two by the steep flight of steps leading down to the white wooden gate and a ragged hawthorn hedge. It was roughly terraced with vertical slabs of stone supporting the soil and on each of three levels there were patches of grass edged with herbaceous plants. The top level either side of the steps was a smoother lawn that Joshua and Poopie had tamed in the first week and kept in order ever since. On the lawn to the south of the steps, Wimpey had a swing put up for her by Joshua on the stout bough of a sycamore tree. Miss Quigley also favoured the south side of the garden, away from the windows of the house. Here she would set up her easel and paint the moors and the hills and the country roads that went on and on forever.

"At least you like it here," said Pilbeam one day as she looked over Miss Quigley's shoulder. The artist shrugged her shoulders and pressed her lips together as one who could say more but wouldn't. Pilbeam was used to Miss Quigley's odd manner. She never quite understood, but she accepted her oddness as normal.

"Miss Quigley's made a beautiful landscape picture," said Pilbeam to Appleby, attempting to rouse the latter from a lethargy that had set in rather badly over the past few weeks.

"Has she?" said Appleby listlessly.

They were sitting on a bench in front of the drawing-room window. It was the beginning of August. The day was warm and sultry.

"Come and see it," said Pilbeam.

"Can't be bothered," said Appleby. "You go if you like."

Pilbeam looked annoyed.

"Listen, Appleby," she said, "we all wish we were back home. You're not the only one who doesn't like it here. Try to make the best of things. Mother does. Granny does. And Miss Quigley."

"Miss Quigley's enjoying herself," said Appleby looking across to the far lawn where Hortensia was absorbed in her work. "She likes it here. You can tell. All that beautiful landscape! She'll be fancying herself as Constable or Gainsborough or some such. Well, let her get on with it. I'm not going to drool over her efforts."

"You're a spiteful little madam," said Pilbeam. "I really don't know why I bother with you."

Pilbeam got up and went over to see the artist at work. Appleby gave a sigh and then trailed after her older sister.

Pilbeam took up her usual position by Miss Quigley's right shoulder. She looked again at the painting. And gasped.

"What on earth did you do that for?" she asked, astounded at what she saw.

Wimpey, hearing the tone of Pilbeam's voice, slid off her swing and came to look. Appleby came up behind her and stared at the painting. All she could do was echo Pilbeam's words, "Why did you do that, Miss Quigley? You've spoilt it."

"I don't think 'spoilt' is the right word, my dear," said Miss Quigley with a glint in her eye and in her voice. "I don't feel as if I've spoilt it."

The landscape of the day before, a sort of magical exaggeration of the real view in front of her, was still there, but now it was merely the background for a very intricate and precisely detailed black line-drawing of a three-storey house with two attic windows in the roof.

"It's home!" cried Wimpey. "It's our house in Brocklehurst Grove!"

It was!

In every tiny detail, perfectly remembered, from the chimney pots to the wrought-iron gate, it was an exact picture of Number 5 Brocklehurst Grove.

"Why?" asked Pilbeam, trying to make some sense of it.

"It is my version of line-and-wash," said Hortensia with a bitter little smile. "The wash is where I am. The line is where I dearly long to be."

Wimpey did not understand. Pilbeam understood. Appleby understood heart and soul.

"I know what you mean, Miss Quigley," she said. "I know exactly what you mean."

Miss Quigley looked satisfied. She turned on Pilbeam and in a very schoolmistressy voice she said, "Don't ever say I like it here. I look out over those bleak moors and get weary of seeing nothing but earth and sky, day in, day out. I am not a countrywoman. That is something I have learnt."

Googles, lying in the carrycot beside her nanny's easel, heard the tone of voice and felt disturbed. She began to cry, at first whimpering and then settling for a full-blast bellow.

"There, there, my love," said Hortensia going to pick up her charge and comfort her. "Poor lamb! You don't like it here either. No park, no shops, no life at all . . ."

Wimpey went back and sat on the swing. Her older sisters sat down on the grass beside her, looking disconsolately at the world around them. On the moor, some distance away, a small flock of mangy-looking sheep plodded round aimlessly.

"Little BoPeep has lost her sheep," sang Wimpey as she swung higher and higher.

"With sheep like those," said Appleby, eyeing the animals, "I am not surprised. If I had to look after that lot, I'd want to lose them too."

"Stop it," said Pilbeam. "You sound feeble. Albert's coming down tomorrow. Maybe he'll take us for a drive."

20

The Hundred Steps

Hortensia Quigley took to heart Pilbeam's words about being feeble. She was a woman with iron in her soul. If yearning for Castledean could be thought of as feebleness, she was determined to do her bit to overcome it. That the words had been directed at Appleby made no difference. Hortensia always saw nuances of meaning even where there were none.

The next day was bright but breezy. Hortensia put Googles into a big perambulator that must have stood in the cloak-room for many, many years. The wheels were large with rusty spokes. The hood had been patched on the corners. The boat-shaped body, slung high above coiled springs, was painted dark blue and patterned with a white line that followed its shape. Hortensia gave it a very thorough clean out and replaced the ancient pillows and covers with Googles's own.

"There," she said. "Now we shall go for a nice little walk."

She pushed the pram along the path in front of the house to the track at the far end that led down from the stables to the road. It was steep and uneven and not worthy of being called a drive.

Hortensia stood at the top looking out over the lovely, lonely countryside. The breeze blew round her, ruffling her fine, thin hair. From her handbag she took a chiffon scarf and tied it securely over her head and under her chin. She hooked the bag onto the pram handle. Then she set off down the slope.

She was wearing the same large-buckled brown leather shoes with stumpy heels that she'd had on the day Albert first saw her. She was not a countrywoman. They were not country shoes. As she went down towards the road, gripping the pram handle tightly and putting one foot gingerly in front of the other, disaster struck. One stumpy heel caught in a rut. Miss Quigley lost her balance. And the pram careered away down the hill with Googles letting out a scream of terror.

Another even larger rut bumped the pram up in the air and bounced the baby out onto the ground. The pram continued down the slope to the road and across into the moor where it turned over on its side and spilt out all the fresh clean covers.

Hortensia was horrified as she saw it all happen. She got up and staggered and stumbled to the bottom of the path where her beloved charge was lying face down and perfectly still.

She sat on the grass verge beside the baby. Gently and fearfully she picked her up and sat her on her knee. Googles was absolutely rigid, her arms and legs stiff, her back unbending. The perfect yellow curl that always graced the middle of her forehead was straggling down over her flat little baby nose. Her eyes, hazel flecked with gold that usually flashed and gleamed, were clouded over.

In the hawthorn hedge a bird was singing.

Hortensia hugged the baby tightly and felt a wave of

despair sweep over her. But not for long. This was Hortensia Quigley who had lived for forty years in a cupboard. This was Hortensia Quigley who painted the most beautiful pictures. This was Hortensia Quigley, the best nanny in the world.

She stood up. Following some strange instinct that would not have worked with a human child, she held Googles by the feet and swung her very gently and rhythmically from side to side. At first the tiny figure just went with the rhythm, dead and unresisting. But within minutes Googles began to move her arms and struggle to free her feet. Then she yelled loud enough to startle the bird in the bush. It flew up and circled busily in the sky.

Hortensia turned Googles the right way up and cuddled her till the crying stopped.

"Now," she said, "we must go home."

The pram on the moor was her next objective. She carried Googles over to it, smoothed out one of the covers and laid her down on it. She righted the pram and gave a stern, warning look at a sheep that was straying too near. Next she put the pillows and covers in their proper place, but was puzzled to find that the righted pram had a decided tilt. Investigation proved that the wheel under one side of the hood had fallen off. Hortensia was dismayed but not defeated. She soon found that the wheel would not go back on. So she hooked it onto the handle beside her handbag. It never occurred to her to leave the pram in the field. That would have been disgracefully improvident. But to take a three-wheeled pram up the steep track, especially for someone wearing shoes with a broken heel, would be asking for trouble.

Hortensia viewed the house, standing there against the sky, high as an eagle's nest. A short way down the road was the white wooden gate leading to the hundred steps. And Hortensia knew what had to be done.

She lifted Googles up off the cover and tucked her carefully into the pram. Then she wheeled the vehicle awkwardly along the road to the gate, opened it, and set herself to tackle the herculean task of climbing backwards up the steps pulling the pram, on its two good wheels, up after her. She counted every step.

"My goodness! Whatever have you done to yourself?" exclaimed Vinetta when she saw her friend emerging onto the top lawn looking distraught and bedraggled. Hortensia explained badly and all in a rush, but Vinetta understood and was very sympathetic.

Between them, the two women settled the baby down and put the pram away.

"I'm so sorry," said Hortensia, "and so ashamed. It was shocking. It should never have happened. I am a stupid woman. How can you ever trust me again?"

Vinetta put her arm round Hortensia's narrow shoulders.

"I trust you, Hortensia Quigley, more than anyone on this earth. It was an accident. It was an emergency, but you coped. That was what really mattered."

They were sitting on the sofa in the drawing room. Outside the sun was still shining. Inside the gloom that never left the house belied the time of day.

"I don't know how you managed to climb those hundred steps pulling that monstrous pram," said Vinetta.

"There weren't a hundred," said Hortensia. "Only fifty-eight. A hundred is an exaggeration. But fifty-eight was quite enough. We are prisoners here, Vinetta. We'll never be able to go out again."

21

The Night Rider

Soobie appeared to settle well enough in his new surroundings. It was hard to tell. Soobie rarely looked happy in any circumstances. He had a solemn, sensible, very blue face with silver eyes full of hidden wisdom and maybe hidden hurt. He played chess with Albert and showed some quiet enjoyment in beating him, though it was never an entirely one-sided game. Albert was good. Soobie was better. Some games lasted for more than one visit. Between times, Soobie mostly sat in the library and read. This was truly the quiet part of the house, in the north-west corner, well away from all of the other lived-in rooms. And when the door was shut nobody, not even Albert, intruded.

Soobie would stretch out on the sofa and either read or look disconsolately out at the landscape. Appearances are deceptive. Soobie had not settled into his new environment at all. The blue-striped suit he wore was his one-and-only. In forty years it had been renewed twice and each new suit had been a faithful copy of the one before. So with the view from his window. The bay window at Brocklehurst Grove, the wrought-iron gates, the square with its statue of Matthew James, and the busy road beyond – these were what Soobie wanted, for no other reason than that they had always been his. The view from Comus House of the distant hills and wide, wild stretches of moorland was unendurably empty and lonely and unfamiliar.

Worse still, the one ride on the scooter, whizzing round the stableyard, had reached something deep in Soobie's soul that he had never suspected was there. It went completely contrary to his wish for sameness. Part of him wanted to get on that bike and ride over hill and down dale. His hatred of change and his paradoxical yearning for adventure had this in common – they both made him miserable.

One afternoon in September, Soobie prowled round the house like a cat in search of a comfortable corner. The view from the library was getting on his nerves. His bedroom was full of unfriendly furniture that had belonged to strangers. Nowhere in that house was right. He caught sight of his sisters out in the front garden, looking more at home than he ever could. (But appearances are deceptive!) He could hear his mother and grandmother quietly arguing in the breakfast-room. Miss Quigley and her charge were in the drawing-room. Hortensia was very earnestly engaged in painting a miniature on an oval piece of glass.

Soobie went along the narrow passage that led to the back door. He went out into the yard and crossed to the stables, passing Poopie who was building a camp on top of the well.

"Do you want a game?" asked Poopie hopefully. It was not a stupid question. Soobie could be quite kind about playing with his younger brother. And the best of playing with Soobie was that he took it all very seriously, regarding the game of soldiers more as a mathematical problem than a silly pretend. But not today.

"No," said Soobie, "not today. Some other time."

Poopie said no more and went back to his army. Soobie went into the stable and sat astride the scooter. Without thinking, he took the helmet and put it on his head. Without any real idea of what he intended to do, he checked the petrol, got up and added more from the can Albert had used. Then he wheeled the scooter out into the path.

It was at that point that the demon took over. The yearning for adventure came bubbling to the surface and Soobie free-wheeled down to the road and then started the engine. He did not know where he was going or why. But he was off and away. Not too fast, and never reckless, but feeling an amazing joy as he travelled the country roads.

At a remote garage he stopped and bought more fuel. The woman in the kiosk gave him a funny look. Helmet and goggles covered his blue face. Gloves hid his blue hands. But his suit resembled a pair of pyjamas more than anything else. Still, she thought, takes all sorts to make a world.

It was dusk when Soobie stopped, propped the scooter against a tree, and sat down to rest. Odd, creaky, squeaky noises disturbed him. A fox shot off across the road in front of him. Soobie looked at the sky which was a luminous purple-grey and becoming darker by the minute. It was no use. Whatever the questions were that his peculiar soul kept asking, a scooter ride along country lanes was not going to provide any answers. Why am I here? Because I'm not there.

He thought of trying to find his way back to Brocklehurst Grove. Not impossible. There was a map in the saddlebag. Roads have sign posts. He still had enough money to buy more petrol. Yet there was something wrong with that idea.

He thought of his mother back at Comus House, counting her sheep and finding one missing. It was unfair. She had suffered once before, when Appleby had run away from home. He would not, could not, cause her suffering like that again. She might already have missed him. She might already be worried. He would not prolong her agony.

So, with a sigh and a groan, he pulled himself up off the damp earth, mounted the scooter and set off for Comus House. It was some miles away, and there were many twists and turns in the road, but Soobie did not need the map. He was observant and careful and he knew the way he had come.

He was almost within sight of home and had no more than two miles to cover when the accident happened. It was not his fault. A farm truck pulled suddenly out of a gateway. Its driver was less careful than usual. It was after nine o'clock at night in a very quiet spot. He had not expected there to be any other vehicle on that stretch of road.

Soobie saw him just in time to swerve madly. To keep full control of the bike was impossible. It keeled over and Soobie sprawled in the road. The driver of the truck stopped and jumped out.

"Where the hell did you come from?" he yelled, panicking in case he had hurt the bike-rider and anxious to avoid being blamed.

A dazed Soobie pulled himself hastily to his feet and picked up the scooter.

"I'm all right," he said wildly. "Perfectly all right. No harm done."

"Are you sure?" asked the man, showing decent concern now that he knew he was not being held responsible.

Soobie wheeled the scooter forward into the road, ready to depart. The headlamps of the truck shone on his blue suit. The left trouser leg was ripped and his blue limb was clearly visible. So what did the man see? A very odd character wearing helmet and goggles, large driving gloves, and a pair of tattered, striped pyjamas over what looked like long dark-blue underwear.

"Blimey!" said the man, laughing nervously. "You do see some sights! Does your mother know you're out, sonny?"

Soobie looked down at his blue leg and felt unbearably embarrassed. He jumped onto the scooter and rode away as fast as he could.

He had not been missed at Comus House. Vinetta did not count her sheep as meticulously as all that! But he *was* spotted returning.

Tulip had gone to check that the children had shut the back door. They were in bed by then and Tulip was about to settle down for the night, whether to sleep or knit depended on the state of her insomnia. Every night she checked the doors. This was, after all, the country. There were mice behind the wainscots in Comus House. She knew that already. It was important that no other members of the animal kingdom should be allowed to invade.

The door was shut, but Tulip decided to have one last look out at the night. One of the stable doors was flapping open. With a tut, Tulip made her way across the yard to close it. It was then that she saw Soobie pushing the bike up the path.

"Where have you been with that?" she asked.

"Nowhere," said Soobie crossly. It was perfectly true. He had been nowhere.

Tulip looked at him more closely.

"What on earth has happened to your trouser leg?"

"It's torn," said Soobie.

"How?" asked his grandmother.

"Mind your own business," said Soobie in a surly voice. It was not his normal way of speaking to anybody, let alone his grandmother. But he was angry, and she was there.

Tulip was amazed, infuriated, and for a moment completely winded, gasping for something to say.

"How dare you talk like that to me!" she said at last. "You forget who I am! I don't know what your mother will say when she sees the state you are in. You won't be telling her to mind her own business when you want those trousers cleaned and mended."

"I'll mend them myself," said Soobie, becoming entrenched in his anger. "I don't need anybody to do anything for me."

He put the scooter away, then slammed the garage door and went off into the house without another word or a look. To say that Tulip was livid would be an understatement.

Vinetta would have understood him. Tulip, set in her ways, bound by old rules, did not.

22

Humiliation

The next day Soobie was still angry with everything and everybody. Most of all he was angry with himself. It became a matter of pride to mend his own trouser leg and dust off as much of the dirt as he could. Whenever he felt confused as to whose fault it was that he was a misfit in a marvellous world he always tried to contain his misery by concentrating on something immediate and doable. It was a trick he had learnt long ago.

There was no one in the drawing-room. That was to be expected in the mornings. Soobie found his mother's small workbox on the sideboard where she usually kept it now. From it he took a needle and a bobbin of blue thread. Then he went to the armchair by the window. It had its back to the room and when seated in it one could stay there undetected.

Soobie had no regard for Tulip's often quoted old wives' tale about "sewing sorrow to oneself". He bent over his knee and, holding the cloth away from his leg as much as he could, began painstakingly to sew the tear in his trousers. It was not easy and he was not neat. Tulip would have called it "dog's tooth" stitching.

After about twenty minutes, Pilbeam came into the room and picked up a magazine she had left on the sofa. Soobie was aware of her coming and going, but he gave no sign and she did not realise he was there.

Another ten minutes went by before Vinetta came in and sat by the fire. Tulip joined her. She had already complained bitterly to her daughter-in-law about Soobie's rudeness of the night before. It was not a subject she was going to let drop.

"Are you going to speak to him?" she demanded of Vinetta.

"Yes," said Vinetta. "I will. I have already told you I will."

"When?"

"Some time today. I'll go along to the library and have a quiet word."

"That's more than he had with me," said Tulip. "A word, yes, but far from quiet. And very, very rude. Do you think I'd have allowed Joshua to talk to me like that when he was his age? You have no control over those children, Vinetta. Nobody has. And it's your fault. You've spoilt them."

Soobie was sitting all this while overhearing all that was said. He did not want to be a listener but he did not want to join in either. So he shrank down and looked at the mend in his trousers. Beauty, as Sir Magnus was wont to say, is in the eye of the beholder. Soobie thought he had made a reasonably good job of that repair.

Vinetta winced at Tulip's words but she held back her anger.

"They have to control themselves," she said. "What they say or do is their responsibility."

"And where they go and what they wear," said Tulip, working herself up. "Soobie wouldn't be allowed across the doors if he were my son. He is alien to us, never mind

117

outsiders. It would help if you could persuade him to wear clothes like other people. What does he look like going around day in day out in what you could best describe as a pair of crumpled striped pyjamas? He's a freak. He's nothing but a freak."

Vinetta felt crushed and angry.

"What about yourself?" she snapped. "You're never seen without a pinny."

"It is not always the same pinny," said Tulip haughtily, "and it is never other than crisp and clean. But I see how it is. You are sticking up for them as usual. And much thanks you get! You are a doormat as far as your children are concerned. You'll never learn."

Vinetta managed to remain outwardly calm.

"If I am a doormat," she said, "at least I am useful."

Then suddenly they were gone their separate ways and the room was empty.

Empty except for Soobie, hidden in the armchair. Soobie the freak, in his badly-mended trousers, nursing a broken heart.

He went along the dark, winding passage to the library and lay down on the sofa to die.

23

Poopie

Poopie Mennym had the innate ability to make himself at home anywhere. And the stable-garage was not just anywhere. It was a huge enclosed space where battles could be fought and won. Hector, his favourite Action Man, could hide with his troops under the wooden staircase that led up to the loft. Basil, the enemy leader, a vicious character who had lost half of his left arm in some old war, would unwittingly lead his men into an ambush. Ignorant armies clashed by night! Tanks and jeeps zoomed across the concrete part of the floor till they bumped into the flagstones at the rear.

It startled the rabbit.

All that noise and commotion and there in the back of the stables was a young rabbit with a limp, injured front paw, just longing for peace and quiet. It cowered back into the corner. The first Poopie knew of its existence was when a shaft of light coming through one of the shutters caught just a glimpse of movement and the flicker of a frightened eye.

Poopie went cautiously to investigate. He remembered the rat that had once gnawed his father's leg in the warehouse where he worked.

"It's a rabbit!" he exclaimed with a mixture of feelings of which the strongest was delight. He was born knowing what a rabbit was. Everybody is!

He stooped down and gingerly touched the little rabbit's head. It was warm and furry and bony. Poopie could feel the bones in its little skull. The rabbit froze. It made no attempt to escape. Very soon it must have come to the conclusion that the cloth hand was friendly, or at least harmless. It looked up hopefully into Poopie's bright blue eyes, wide with wonder under the yellow fringe.

"I won't hurt you," said Poopie gently. "You are my rabbit. I'm going to look after you."

He sneaked into the house and brought out an old tracksuit top. He filled a soup plate with water from the kitchen tap. From the side-garden he took some lettuce leaves.

"There," he said, settling the rabbit on the tracksuit top and putting the plate of water in front of it. "Now you can be comfortable."

He sat on the floor beside his new pet and nervously, held out a piece of lettuce leaf. The little animal bit on it immediately and Poopie hastily drew back his hand.

It was wonderful. It was even better than watching Albert eat. The leaf disappeared like magic and the rabbit was ready for more.

"I'll call you Andy Black," said Poopie. "You can be my friend. I'll let you play with me. You can have a ride on the tank."

That never happened. First, Poopie was still too cautious to lift Andy Black right out of the corner. Secondly, Wimpey came looking for her brother and spotted something he had missed.

"What you doing in there?" demanded Wimpey from

the open doorway. She had her skipping-rope in her hand. Outside, the sun was shining.

"Come on in," said Poopie eagerly. "Come and see Andy Black. But don't tell any of the others. It's a secret."

Wimpey ran across the concrete floor onto the flagstones. The stable was very gloomy. Wimpey's eyes adjusted to the change in light and she looked down wonderingly at the rabbit.

"He's not black," she said. "He's brown."

"I never said he was black," said Poopie loftily. "His name is Andy Black. Black is a name as well as a colour. You could be Wimpey Black, if you weren't Wimpey Mennym."

Wimpey looked more closely at the rabbit.

"He's hurt his paw," she said. "That is why he hasn't run away. You can't keep him a secret, Poopie. You'll have to tell Mother. She is the one who mends things."

Vinetta came to the stables and cleansed and bandaged the hurt paw, but she looked worried.

"That's the best I can do," she said, "but I think maybe he should be taken to a vet. We'll have to ask Albert when he comes."

Albert came the next day. It was a Tuesday. He brought Joshua to stay the night and was to take him back to Castledean in time for work on Wednesday evening. The Range Rover had proved very useful. Joshua usually managed to pay his family a visit once a fortnight or so. It was a poor substitute for having his whole family at home in Castledean, but it was better than nothing.

"I don't know about a vet," said Albert. "I don't really know very much about animals. It looks all right to me."

"Did you never have a pet when you were young?" asked Vinetta to jog his memory.

Albert grinned.

"I once kept a worm in a shoe box!"

Joshua liked the look of the rabbit – a nice, quiet creature. "I'll make a hutch for it," he said kindly. "I'll bring it down the next time I come."

"That won't make any difference to its paw," said Vinetta, still worried. "We'll ask Magnus," she said at last.

They got a large cardboard box from a cupboard in the house, carefully tipped Andy Black into it and proceeded upstairs to Granpa's room.

The old man was sitting propped up in the four-poster bed. The bed curtains, washed and ironed, were tied back with a cord, one to each bed-post. The pillows behind his head were very old and stiff, but the pillowcases were still white with deep frills round the edges. Granpa was wearing a crimson night-cap that Tulip had found in the dressing-table drawer. Magnus, alone of all the household, even including Albert, looked a real match for the house. The others were anachronisms.

"No need for a vet," pronounced Sir Magnus after he had peered at the animal over the edge of the box. "You've made a good job of that paw, Vinetta. It'll heal in no time."

"What about a hutch?" asked Joshua.

"No," said his father. "All that animal needs is some straw bedding in the stables. He's a wild creature, not a pet."

Sir Magnus looked down at Poopie.

"You'll have to keep changing the bedding. Rabbits can get dirty and smelly."

"What if he runs away when his paw gets better?" asked Poopie anxiously.

"If he does, he does," said his grandfather. "By the time his paw's better, he'll know you. He'll know it's you that's looked after him. Even a rabbit should have enough sense to know what side his bread's buttered on."

It was an alien pearl of wisdom. Only Albert had any idea what it meant.

"Come on, Andy Black," said Poopie. Throwing caution to the winds, he lifted the rabbit out of the box and hugged it to his chest.

24

Allenbridge Market

"I'll take you both to Allenbridge," said Albert. "It's market day. You'll like it."

Poor Albert! He tried to sound hopeful but he was well aware that the family were fish out of water in the countryside. He hadn't seen Soobie for the past three weeks but was careful never to mention it. He knew that Wimpey had bad dreams and slept with the light on all night. The dark passages of the house filled her with fear. The hoot of an owl would send her screaming to Vinetta. As for the older girls, they were obviously totally bored, especially Appleby who would not even take comfort in books.

Albert's own life had become dreamlike. He was back at work, of course. The vacation was over, but he still spent as much time as he could toing and froing between Durham, Castledean and Comus House.

"Dr Pond," one of his first-year students had asked in the middle of last term, "do you believe in the paranormal?"

He had blinked at the girl and looked guilty.

"I mean," she had continued, "do you believe in reincarnation? Do you think that people from history could be living now? Kings coming back as road-sweepers, beggars returning as millionaires?"

"A nice thought, Lorna," Albert had said, smiling, "but I don't think it could work quite like that! If you carried it to a logical conclusion, you'd end up with too many kings and not enough road-sweepers!"

He was relieved that the girl was just burbling on the way his students sometimes did. For a moment he had thought she'd divined the terrible tangle he had got himself into caring for Kate's creations.

He had checked several times on what was happening in Brocklehurst Grove. It was now nearly four months since the family had left, and there seemed to be no progress at all towards saving the Grove, despite valiant efforts to gain public support. Albert had rung Anthea once at the gallery number and been told cryptically, "Wait and see, Albert. The Fryers are not easily beaten."

It was Albert's best hope. But in the meantime he had to try to get the Mennyms settled down, just in case the worst should come to the worst.

Appleby heard the magic word 'market' and was keen to go. Castledean Market, row upon row of stalls with all sorts of goods on display, had been one of her favourite places. Allenbridge Market should be interesting.

"I'm sitting in the front seat," she said. Albert gave Pilbeam a rueful, apologetic smile. Pilbeam smiled back and shrugged her shoulders.

"I don't mind taking a back seat," she said. "Let her have her own way. She usually does."

Appleby said grudgingly, "You can have the front seat on the way back, if you really want it."

The little town of Allenbridge was twenty miles north-west of Comus House. The Range Rover crossed the humped-back bridge and went up the narrow street to a clock tower that stood right in the middle of the road which, of necessity, widened at that point.

"We go right here," said Albert. "The marketplace is just round the next corner."

"Is that it?" asked Appleby in disgust. There were no more than a dozen stalls. A fête on the local cricket field back home would have made a better showing. People in the square seemed already to be eyeing the Range Rover and wondering who the visitors might be.

Pilbeam said quietly, "It was a nice thought, Albert, but I don't think we'd dare get out here. We'd be too conspicuous, especially arriving in the Range Rover. It's a small place. Everybody obviously knows everybody else."

Appleby flopped back in her seat sulkily. "Some use this is," she said. "I wish I'd never come."

"I'll take you up to Scotland," said Albert desperately. "We'll have a nice long drive and I'll get you home by ten. That's the time I told your mother we'd be back. It's only ten past two now, so we'll have bags of time."

Where time was concerned, Albert always tended to err on the side of optimism.

They drove on. There were fields and hills and a long stretch of forest. It was a beautiful golden afternoon, better than many a summer's day.

The signpost at the road-side told them that they were crossing the border.

"Beautiful, isn't it?" said Albert.

"Lovely," said Pilbeam from the back seat.

"It's no different from England," said Appleby. "Just the

same thing over and over again. Fields and trees and more fields."

She said it spitefully. By this time she had made up her mind to see no good in anything. She had expected to rummage in a market and nothing else would do.

Albert gave her a sidelong glance.

"What did you expect?" he said. "Tartan hills?"

"Or streets paved with bagpipes," Pilbeam added with a giggle.

Appleby was not amused. She gave them both a look of fury, and she sat in her seat and she smouldered, she smouldered and smouldered and smouldered!

"I want to go home," she said.

"That's where we're going," said Albert as he turned to the south.

"No it's not," said Appleby, just about spitting out the words. "We're going to Comus House. That's not home. It never will be."

"Ungrateful brat!" said her sister, and thereafter they were silent.

Albert drove carefully along the narrow country roads. He broke no speed limits and when darkness came he was extra wary of every bump and bend. There were, however, one or two slight hitches.

"I thought we would be too far west to see the sea," said Pilbeam after they had travelled for some while.

"The sea?" said Albert, looking across to his left.

"No," said Pilbeam. "Over there, on our right. I can barely see it, but I am sure there are lights on a ship out there."

Albert gave a cry of dismay.

"We're going north-east," he said. "I must have taken a wrong turning. We should be going south."

It was after midnight when they arrived at Comus House. There were lights in most of the windows — Vinetta's idea. The curtains were all open and the lights shone out like a beacon across the countryside. Only the library and Granpa's room were left in darkness.

"If they're lost," Vinetta said, "they'll see the lights and Albert will surely recognise the road."

Tulip's look was one of exasperation but she said nothing. It was impossible to persuade this daughter-in-law of hers to ease up on the worrying. So the lights burned on wastefully for hours.

"Where on earth have you been all this time?" Vinetta demanded when they returned at last. "You've had us terrified in case something had happened."

In the loft at Bedemarsh Farm, more than seven miles away, Billy Maughan and his friend Joe Dorward had just finished a feast of crisps, pop and chocolate biscuits. If Billy's dad had known they were up there, there'd have been the devil to pay. It was a good hiding place, above the west wing of the old farmhouse and accessible by an iron-rail fire escape. If Joe's mum had known he was so far from home at that time of night, she would have been frantic with worry, but she didn't know and she was fast asleep in the room above the bar at the village pub.

"I'd best be going now," said Joe. "Let's have another look at our fireworks, then I'll be off."

Billy carefully opened the brown-painted metal 'tatchy' case that had belonged to his maternal great-grandfather. The name THOMAS MACRAE was scratched right across the inside of the lid in huge twiggy letters that looked like runes.

It was a safe place to store their secret hoard of bangers, whizzers and rocketry.

"Your dad would skin you if he knew you had that lot up here," said Joe looking down at his younger, smaller friend. Billy was ten years old, but he was small for his age and very slightly built. His wispy ginger hair and pouchy grey eyes made him look wizened. Joe was tall, dark, handsome and twelve.

"Well, he don't know and he's not goin' to know, less you tell'm," said Billy smartly. He might be small but he had spirit.

They were about to have a scuffle when they decided to play secret agents instead. Billy had an old pair of binoculars which he used for watching the countryside in the wee small hours, hoping to spot poachers, smugglers or even villains carrying a body out to a secret burial. There never was anybody, but you could always pretend. They took turns looking.

Seven miles to the north-west was Tidy Hill, high and round-topped, the site for the bonfire.

"It'll be better than ever this year," said Joe. "Jimmy Reed and Geoff Martin've been up there and they say the pile of rubbish is the highest they've ever seen and there's three weeks to go yet."

Billy took his turn with the binoculars. He swivelled round to the south and there, four or five miles south of Tidy Hill, was Comus House, lit up brightly against the dark sky. Billy nearly dropped the binoculars in his excitement.

"There's nobody lives there," he said. "Nobody's lived there for years. Look, Joe, look."

"There's somebody there now," said Joe in a waspishly mysterious voice, "and it's my betting they're up to no good. We'll have to investigate this one, Watson."

"Yes, Holmes," said Billy, in a rather poor imitation of his friend's sinister tones. Playing at the game they called 'Holmes and Watson', the boys had investigated more than one 'case', but this looked above average interesting.

The lights at Comus House went out. Joe consulted his very special watch and, in his own voice, said, "Crumbs! It's nearly one o'clock. I'll never be able to get up in the morning! It's all right for you, Billy Maughan, all you have to do is sneak back to your room. I've over a mile to walk before I get to mine."

"But we will investigate it sometime," said Billy hopefully.

"Sometime," said his friend, "but not in the foreseeable, leastways not at this time of night."

With a quick "See ya", he ran out and down the fire-escape into the darkness.

25

Sir Magnus

"This can never be home to us," said Sir Magnus yet again as Tulip opened the curtains on a raw October morning. The fine spell had passed and winter looked like setting in early. Tulip pursed her lips and went on with tying up the drapes round the four-poster bed.

"Well?" said Magnus. "What do you think we should do?"

"This is a stupid conversation," said his wife. "We've had it every morning for weeks. There's nothing we can do. We'll just have to get used to it."

Magnus gave her one of his bleakest looks.

"We're town sparrows, Tulip," he said, "not country crows. A few more weeks of this and we'll all be dead."

Tulip sat beside the bed and put her small hand into his large mittened palm.

"That's putting it a bit strong," she said. "I do know how you feel, but try to be more positive. What's so special about the town anyway? When we were there, you never went out. You never stirred from your bed. The world outside might have been anywhere, town, country or Timbuctoo. Think of it that way. Try to pretend that this is Brocklehurst Grove and that Castledean is just outside the window."

Sir Magnus sat up very straight, clenched both fists by his sides and said, "Do not humour me. I will not be humoured. I know what I know. The main street ran past Brocklehurst Grove. The sky was never totally dark. The town lights gave it a night-long glow."

"And what did you see of it?" said Tulip.

"It doesn't matter. I knew it was there. The spirit of the place was different. The light that filtered through the curtains had a different glow. Here the light of day is cold and blank, the night is dead. I hate it. It gives me claustrophobia."

"Agoraphobia," Tulip corrected him. "You have a fear of open spaces."

"Agora – you would know if you had studied Greek – is a market place. I have no fear at all of marketplaces. What I dread is being imprisoned by fields."

Tulip decided to try another way to pacify him.

"The view from the back of the house might please you better," she said. "Put on your slippers and dressing gown. Let's go and see the view from Appleby's room. Hers is the best. She specially chose it for the view. But if you like it, we'll persuade her to change over."

Tulip fully knew what 'persuade' meant when talking of Appleby. The bribe would have to be big enough!

Appleby was amazed when she opened her bedroom door and saw her grandparents standing there. Tulip was no real surprise, of course, dressed as usual in her neat dark dress with its lace collar and her blue and white checked apron. But Granpa, resplendent in a dressing gown of dark red velvet trimmed with gold braid and wearing a very large pair of green leather slippers on his purple feet, looked fantastic. The walking-stick he leant on was not the smooth cane that had stood by his bed at Brocklehurst Grove. It was a stout, gnarled, country model that went with the house.

"Can we come in?" asked Tulip politely. "I'd like to show Granpa the view from your window. He's feeling a bit down."

Appleby looked at the two of them and shrugged her shoulders.

"Come in and see the view, if that's all you want," she said. "It's not much to write home about, supposing we had a home. Still, it's not moorland, and there are no scruffy sheep."

Comus House was built on the ridge of a scarp. The familiar west side, at the front, fell steeply down to the moor road. To the east, from the upstairs windows, one could see the old stone wall, and, over the wall, ten or twenty miles of gently sloping land. Meadow gave way to crop fields, stubble now after the harvest. In the distance were well-scattered clusters of farm buildings. To the north there were even signs of a village, a church spire so far away that it looked no bigger than a pencil point. And, best of all, due east, almost parallel to the horizon and very near to it, was the main road.

Appleby was eager to point this out to her grandfather.

"Look," she said. From the window ledge she took a pair of bright yellow binoculars. They were not much better than a child's toy, but their magnification was sufficient to bring the road near enough for them to make out the dual carriage-way and the vehicles travelling north and south.

"We live down there," said Appleby pointing to the south. "I've looked it up on the map."

"No we don't," said Magnus harshly. "We live here. And I can't see any prospect of us living anywhere else."

"I know, Granpa," said Appleby. "You hate it here, don't you? I hate it too. I know just how you feel."

Tulip gave her granddaughter a very severe look.

"Stop that. We're very lucky to have this place. We could be much worse off."

"Could we?" said Granpa sourly.

"Yes. We could. What we have to do now is to get used to being countryfolk. What can't be cured must be endured."

Faced with one of his own pearls of wisdom, Magnus thumped his stick on the floor, plodded heavily across the corridor to his own room and settled back in his bed to sulk.

26

The Sorrows of Soobie

After the night ride, and all that followed it, Soobie plummeted into a gloom so deep that nothing would arouse him. The old life was gone, forty years fled away. The new life had given him one adventure which had ended not in triumph but in bitterness and gall. Vinetta had never 'had a word with him' about his rudeness to his grandmother. After the hurtful things Tulip had said she did not feel called upon to do so. That was without even knowing that her beloved son had heard every word.

Tulip had been very frosty for a couple of days, but then her conscience had caught up with her and she was ashamed of some of the things she had said in the heat of the moment. She did not apologise to Vinetta, but she allowed their relationship to return to normal. An unspoken, but well-understood, way of saying sorry.

And all this time, Soobie stayed in the library. It was a small room full of books. Bookshelves covered three of its four walls. In the middle of the fourth wall was a large dormer window, fastened in the middle, that went from the ceiling nearly to the floor. It was curtained in dark green velvet. There were no net curtains and whoever lay on the green plush sofa that faced this window would be able to see far to the west, if he looked. Soobie did not look. He lay on the sofa and he stared, uncaring and unseeing.

"Soobie never comes out of the library now," said Wimpey to Poopie. "I mean – he never ever comes out. He doesn't even go up to bed."

She had braved the long, twisting passage and peeped in once or twice to see her brother, but he had just lain there and taken no notice. Once she had ventured to go up to the sofa and look right in his face. He scowled and Wimpey had retreated.

"It's up to him what he does," said Poopie.

"No it's not," said Wimpey. "He looks dead miserable lying there. I don't want him to be miserable."

"He doesn't care whether you're miserable or not. He's not worth bothering about."

Poopie, truth to tell, was cross with Soobie. He was always cross with anyone who made life feel uncomfortable. He was too young to know his own reasons properly, but he was old enough to feel cross.

Vinetta looked in on Soobie from time to time.

"Those books look interesting," she said. "I'm sure you can't have read all of them."

Soobie ignored her.

Another day, Vinetta brought in a pair of ladders and vigorously cleaned the window.

Soobie twisted round on the sofa and turned his face to the backrest.

"You can see for miles from this window," said Vinetta forlornly to the back of her son's head.

Soobie did not answer.

After trying all sorts of gentle, polite questions and tactics,

Vinetta decided it was time to tackle the problem head on. It was the end of October. Soobie had sulked for weeks. He had even stopped putting in an appearance when Albert came, though they had been in the middle of a long-running game of chess.

"Soobie," she said sharply, "I've had enough of this. What gives you the right to give up? You were my mainstay. I really felt I could depend on you."

"Well, you can't," said Soobie roughly. They were the first words he had spoken in more than a month.

"Why?" asked Vinetta.

"Go away," said Soobie, sounding for all the world like Appleby on a bad day. "What I do is my business. I can't make it plainer than that."

Vinetta waited for Albert to come again.

"You two seemed to get on so well together," she said. "Go and see him, Albert. See if you can coax him round. It breaks my heart knowing that he is just lying there as if he wanted to die."

Albert did not feel at all comfortable about intruding on Soobie. They really were very good friends and Albert felt that their friendship was being used. However, to please Vinetta, who surely deserved some consideration, he went shyly into the little library. He sat down on a stiff-backed armchair to the left of the window. There was a table desk behind the sofa with a seat tucked into it. There was no other furniture in the room.

"This room's a bit Spartan," said Albert. "I hate a room without a fire-place. I wouldn't choose to stay in it for long."

Soobie said nothing. He did not even look up.

"When are we going to finish that game of chess?" asked Albert. "You've got me in a tight spot!"

Soobie did not speak.

Albert felt beaten. The thing on the sofa was a rag doll, a blue rag doll at that. Where was Soobie, the real Soobie, Albert's friend?

"Come on, Soobie," said Albert desperately. "Be yourself. We're all worried about you."

Soobie suddenly sat upright on the sofa and glared at Albert, eyes glinting like steel in an inky-blue face.

"Go away," he said. "Leave me alone."

Then he lay down again and glared straight ahead of him towards, but not at, the window. It was late afternoon. The sky outside was grey and misty.

"Would you like me to close the curtains for you and put on the light?" asked Albert, unwilling to give up.

"No," said Soobie. "Just go away and leave me alone."

Albert got up, stood for a few seconds uncertain what to do, then very reluctantly he left the room.

Vinetta spoke to Pilbeam about her twin's impenetrable gloom.

"I wish there were something I could do," she said. "Can you not speak to him, Pilbeam? Get him to say what's wrong? It surely can't just be homesickness? There has to be more to it than that."

Pilbeam shook her head.

"It's no good, Mother. Albert's tried. If Soobie needs to be alone, he needs to be alone. He has made it quite clear that he doesn't want to be coaxed. Just respect his mood. Let him be. That is the best you can do."

"You talked to Appleby once," said her mother.

"That was different," said Pilbeam. "We are all different. No two people are the same. No two situations are the same."

27

Saving the Grove

The efforts to save the Grove were, as Appleby had predicted, noisy, intrusive, and bathed in publicity. Drowned in publicity almost. Anthea Fryer believed that nothing short of saturation would do. Her father, the TV producer, had slid from one cliché to the next advising full media cover, the glare of the spotlights, words in the right places. But even he did not imagine the things Anthea would get up to.

Troops of Boy Scouts were persuaded to march round carrying posters on sticks and shouting slogans. A juvenile jazz band, glad of the work, gave a concert on the green under the statue of Matthew James. Baton-swinging majorettes chanted:

"We want to save the Grove,
We want to save the Grove,
Ay, Ay, addey oh!
We want to save the Grove."

This was followed by a very vigorous shout:

"What do we want?
What do we want?

We want to save
The Grove!!!"

The batons swung high in the air and were dextrously caught again each time the final word was reached. The local TV station recorded the occasion and actually managed to get a slot for it on the national news.

Anthea herself was interviewed on both TV and radio. A sincere girl, totally dedicated to the one purpose of keeping the bulldozer from the door.

"Surely," said a local councillor on a talk-in programme, "the young lady must know there's no need for all this. There's proper channels. There'll be an Enquiry, an official Enquiry, as always. She can have 'er say at that. They can all have their say. These things take time. Nothing's goin' to happen tomorrow, or the next day for that matter. Take it easy. That's what I say."

Anthea gave him a stern look.

"That's just what you'd like," she said. "A nice quiet Enquiry whilst you're all beavering away in the background getting ready to break the first turf, or whatever it is they do with motorways. Meantime, our houses stand there with a cloud over them and become unsaleable. Then when all but the poor people living here have lost interest the Enquiry will find in favour of the road."

"With all due respect," began the councillor, but Anthea would not allow him to speak.

"Wait," she said. "I haven't finished. That road must be redirected. I even know where it should go. You may have seen my plan. The decision to save our street must be made now, not next year or the year after that. We're not waiting for phase two or phase three. We're pushing for an immediate withdrawal of the threat hanging over us."

"Perhaps Councillor Eliot would like one last word," said the programme's chairman with an anxious look at the studio clock.

He didn't quite get that last word. The show faded out and the titles came up just as he started to speak.

The wrangling continued. Joshua got used to hearing noises and seeing flashing lights in the street. It made him very uneasy going out to work. There was no back entrance or he would have used it. Where Number 5's garden ended in a thick hedge, another garden began, the long, neglected back garden of one of the old Georgian terrace houses that were being pulled down in the name of progress. They had at one time been superb town houses, but for many years they had been sublet to assorted tenants and allowed to fall into irreversible neglect. Absolutely no one was trying to make any sort of case for their preservation.

After months of arguing, to the surprise of everyone, even the dauntless Anthea, the opposition suddenly collapsed. A new set of plans was drawn up. Brocklehurst Grove was saved. The victory could not be allowed to go unmarked! Anthea Fryer and her loyal supporters saw to that.

BROCKLEHURST GROVE IS SAVED
HIP! HIP! HOORAY!

The letters were bright blue on a gold background. The banner was being fastened ceremoniously into place.

Anthea was sitting on the top rung of a very long ladder tying cords to the base of the chimney pot at Number 9. On another equally long ladder by her side, Bobby Barras, the fire-chief who happened to live at Number 1, was giving assistance and advice. He had tried to persuade Anthea to leave the job to the professionals, but nobody had ever been able to persuade Anthea to do anything.

"Careful now, Miss Fryer. It's all a matter of keeping cool and not looking down. Easy does it."

Anthea gave him a chinny smile.

"Don't you worry yourself, Mr B. I've been up ladders twice the height of this one. There's nothing to it."

It was a Monday afternoon, the first day of November. The light was already beginning to fade, streetlamps were coming on, the cars that jammed the main road had all turned on their headlamps. The crowd that filled the square had umbrellas held up against a thin, cold shower of rain. A television camera was recording the event for the evening news.

Yes, Brocklehurst Grove was well and truly saved. It was not Anthea who had saved it. Her enthusiasm would not have budged That Lot, no matter what she thought. Indirectly though, it *was* the banner that saved the Grove. The first banner.

A lady called Felicity Caxton, who did not even live in Castledean, had seen the banner from the top of a 27 bus. She was a direct descendant of Matthew James Brocklehurst. A bus was not her usual mode of travel, but on a particular Thursday in the middle of August that is where she happened to be. One glimpse of the name Brocklehurst, and the sight of her ancestor seated beneath it, was enough to arouse her interest and indignation. What followed was due entirely to the fact that she and all her many friends and relations belonged to the group known as That Lot. By the beginning of November the plans for the motorway had been changed. The church that was always closed could be demolished instead. The letterbox with the monogram of Queen Victoria would be removed and placed in the Open Air Museum. And everyone could live happily ever after.

By the time Joshua set out for work that Monday evening,

the crowds had dispersed, the carnival was over, it was cold and dark. Only the banner remained. Joshua did not even notice that it was not the same bedraggled sheet of cloth that had been there for weeks.

"Much good a banner will do," he had said to himself more than once as he had trudged his weary way. It is one thing to begrudge speaking to one's nearest and dearest. It is quite another to have no one there to ignore. Joshua was very, very lonely. He loved being a quiet man in a noisy household. That was something he had never known till now. He never ever phoned Vinetta, he did not even know the number, but he was always pleased when she phoned him. Way back in July, as he was leaving for home, Vinetta had insisted upon writing the Comus House number down for him, 'in case of an emergency.' He had nodded absently and slipped it into his coat pocket.

He was sitting in the little office at Sydenham's, quietly smoking his pipe, when suddenly he realised that something that evening had been different. He recalled being at home, half-watching the early evening news on the television.

"That was our street!" he said out loud as light dawned on him. "Our street on the news."

He racked his brains to think further about it – rejoicing they were, that crowd outside, chanting something like "We shall not be moved!" And there were ladders. A close-up of a girl with blonde hair and big teeth waving from a roof top.

Then he remembered leaving the house. No crowds then. The banner was still there, but, surely, it was different – streetlamps, wet rag of a banner, but – yes – it was yellow, not white. Of course! It was yellow. He was sure it was yellow. It was not the same banner.

Putting two and two and two together he managed to make a glorious six.

"They've done it," he cried. "They've saved the Grove. Now we can all settle down at home again."

He made himself a mug of 'cocoa' to celebrate. Port Vale had never had a happier supporter! He never really knew why he supported that particular football team, or where he had acquired their commemorative mug. It was just part of him, an important part.

28

Where's the Scooter?

For Poopie it was a miserable Monday. The rabbit had disappeared from the stable. He had not seen it for three days. One hopeful sign was that something had accepted a free meal of lettuce, carrot and water the night before and Poopie was determined to keep watch in the stable that night. He told his mother all about it.

"I think Andy Black came and had his supper last night, Mum. I'm sure he can't be far away."

Vinetta was concerned when he told her his plan.

"I'll take a sleeping bag and a torch," he said, "and I'll hide behind the scooter and watch. I'll put some food out again. I'm sure he'll come for it."

Vinetta was in the middle of pretending to mix a cake. It was part of her plan for settling in. She would pretend to use the old fire oven, and there were some lovely thick oven gloves she could slot her hands into as she opened the cold-hot door.

She put her earthenware basin down on the kitchen table, a huge thing topped with planks of bare wood. Sitting in the rocking-chair, she drew Poopie down onto a stool beside her. Gently, she tried to explain to him that his hopes were likely to be dashed.

"Even if he does come, Poopie, you can't do much more than say hello. You can't keep him prisoner. He's a little wild animal. You helped him and you loved him and now you'll have to let him go."

Poopie looked woebegone.

"I'd like to see him again, just this once. If I told him that I'd just like him to visit us and he didn't have to stay, he might understand."

Vinetta sighed.

"It might not even be the rabbit that ate the lettuce. It could be anything. It could be mice. It could be a rat."

She shuddered.

"It's Andy Black," said Poopie crossly. "I know it's Andy Black."

Poopie went off with the sleeping bag, the torch and the rabbit's supper to settle himself down for the night. It was six o'clock on Monday evening and already pitch dark. The torch was an old bicycle lamp with a very bright beam. Poopie entered the stable with not a grain of fear. He made his way over to the corner where the scooter was kept.

It wasn't there.

"Mum, Mum, Mum," he yelled running into the kitchen. "The scooter's gone from the stable."

"It can't have done," said Vinetta. "You're just panicking. Come on, I'll come with you and look."

Pilbeam followed them out across the yard. She had come into the kitchen for company. In recent days she had become closer and closer to Vinetta. Appleby was always miserable and Soobie had withdrawn from the world. Pilbeam felt helpless.

The stable doors were wide open. Poopie shone the lamp

all around, up the staircase in the centre, under the staircase, round the walls, everywhere.

"You see," he said, "it's not there. It's not anywhere. Somebody's nicked it."

Vinetta took fright immediately.

"Soobie!" she said. "It has to be Soobie."

Followed by Pilbeam and Poopie, she rushed off into the house, along twisting passages to the library at the north end. She flung open the door. A flood of light from the passage entered the dark room. The curtains were still open but the sky outside was nearly black. On the sofa lay a dark lumpish figure, unmoving, ignoring the commotion.

"Soobie," said Vinetta, relieved that he was still there. "Thank goodness!"

The blue Mennym reluctantly turned his head to peer at the three figures standing in the doorway.

"Go away," he said. "Why can't you just leave me in peace?"

"The scooter's gone from the stable," said Vinetta. "Somebody must have stolen it."

"Well, it wasn't me," said Soobie "So all of you can get out of here and leave me alone. Ask Appleby about it. She has as good a chance of knowing where it is as anybody."

"What makes you say that?" asked his mother, alarmed again.

"She can ride it," said Soobie. "That's all I'm saying."

He felt irritated, as if they were forcing him to break a vow of silence.

"Now go," he said.

But Poopie had already gone. Before Vinetta or Pilbeam could work out the implications, Poopie realised that Appleby had not been seen all day and that the scooter and Appleby had probably disappeared together.

Her room was empty. Her bed was made. The place was in an unusual state of tidiness. Propped up against the dressing-table mirror was a large piece of cardboard with a message written in bright red lipstick:

DON'T BOTHER TO LOOK FOR ME. I NEVER WANT TO SEE COMUS HOUSE AGAIN.

"Mum!" yelled Poopie from the top of the stairs. "Appleby's run away again. She's left a message."

Vinetta dashed up the stairs and into her daughter's room. She read the note and she fainted.

29

On the Road

Appleby *did* know all about scooters, but not even the clever-
est rider knows how to get from A to B along winding
country roads without frequent stops and checks. She found
the map in the saddlebag, just as Soobie had done. It was
old, but adequate.

Her first stop, naturally, was at the petrol station to fill
up the scooter's tank. No problem. As for appearing in
public, the helmet and goggles were a perfect cover-up. And
on such a cold day it was no wonder she paid the bill
without removing her gloves.

"Mind how you go, love," said the motherly woman in
the kiosk. "It's a bit misty. It'd pay you to have your lights
on."

A gentle reminder. It was only three o'clock in the afternoon, but the visibility was not good.

"Thanks," said Appleby, and she wheeled the scooter out
onto the road before pausing to look at her map again. The
scooter was leaning against the garage's low boundary wall.
Appleby sat on the wall and studied the map.

Suddenly a heavy hand gripped her shoulder. She jumped.

"Easy, easy, sweetheart," said a man's voice. "Nobody's going to hurt you. Lost, are you?"

She looked up at him. He had a strange, threatening face. The skin on his cheekbones was stretched and smooth, unhealthily sallow. His eyes were narrow and so light a brown that they were almost colourless. His lank, pale hair was shoulder-length. He was dressed head to foot in black leather. Appleby shivered. It was a very dangerous situation – a quiet time of day, in a quiet place. The nearest living being was the plump woman in the kiosk and she was far enough away to be no deterrent to an assailant.

"You're not afraid of me, are you?" the man said, squeezing her shoulder more tightly. Appleby looked round her wildly. Then she made up her mind. With a swift movement she thrust the map into the scooter's saddlebag. With her right hand she got a tight grip on the handlebar. Then putting her left hand up to her face she pushed up the goggles and stared into the face of the intruder.

The man looked at the glittering green glass beads in the strange cloth face. He let go his grip and staggered backwards. In that moment, Appleby leapt onto the scooter, gave it full throttle and sped away down the road. The man was later to tell the story over and over again to anyone who would listen. Very few believed him, but it gave rise to legends in which Appleby became a zombie, a corpse, a ghost, or a woman without a face.

Eventually, more by luck than anything, she managed to get herself onto the main road. The road was not very busy and visibility was poor. Which was just as well, thought Appleby, because she was not at all sure whether her vehicle was really allowed on this major road. The alternative of staying on minor roads was in some ways inviting, but it would have been slower and was more open to the possibility of getting lost. Road signs on the dual carriageway made it less necessary to stop and check the map. Appleby made her way south.

She reached the recognisable outskirts of Castledean by five-thirty in the evening. Then she dawdled. It was important to arrive at Brocklehurst Grove no sooner than seven-thirty. She wanted to give her father time to be well on his way to work.

It was dark and it was damp, with a thick fog hanging in the air. Appleby wheeled the scooter silently up the garden path and round the back of the house where she left it outside the garden shed. Into the house she went, straight to the kitchen where she took the shed key out of the tea jar. Once the scooter was safely locked away, she sat herself beside the gas fire in the lounge and switched on the television for company. She turned on the standard lamp.

It was bliss. It was comfort. It was warmth. It was home.

The hours of the night sped by. Appleby dozed in the chair by the fire. The first she knew of time was when she heard the clock on the mantelpiece chime six. Six in the morning . . . Father would be home in a couple of hours. She did not want him to find her there.

Like a criminal, she checked the whole room for any clues to her presence. She turned off the lamp and the gas fire. Then she went to hide herself in the attic.

30

Waiting

Poopie threw a tantrum. His yellow hair stood on end, his blue eyes glared. It was late on Monday night, well past his bedtime. Tulip had tucked Wimpey up long ago, but in the commotion of Appleby's disappearance Poopie had been forgotten.

"I hate everybody," he said. "Soobie's horrible. Appleby's horrible. Mum's horrible. And my rabbit's gone for good."

"Go to bed," said Granny Tulip. "You're tired out. You should be asleep by now."

"I'm not tired," he said. "I'm never tired. And I hate you as well."

Pilbeam looked down at him severely.

"Stop that at once," she said, "or I'll shake you."

"Try it on," said Poopie, looking belligerent. "Just try it on."

He sat down on the hall floor and drummed with his heels.

The nursery door opened.

Miss Quigley came out and carefully shut the door behind her.

"Stand up, young man," she said to Poopie in a very crisp voice.

Poopie, startled, stopped drumming and stood up, almost standing to attention like a little soldier.

"Now," said Miss Quigley, "we have had quite enough of this silliness. You will go to your room and go straight to bed."

And he went!

"Thank you, Hortensia," said Tulip as sweetly as she could. "You do have a way with children!"

"Professional," said the nanny, "purely professional."

With that, she returned to the nursery and the child she was paid to look after.

Pilbeam gave her grandmother an amused smile.

"So now we know," she said.

But there were more serious considerations. In the drawing-room on the sofa, Vinetta was lying full length with her head on her arms. She looked ungainly. Her hair was not neat anymore. Her dress was crumpled.

Pilbeam tried to think of something to say and couldn't. She sat on an armchair beside the sofa and waited.

Tulip came in.

"Come on, Vinetta," she said. "This is doing no good. Pull yourself together."

"I can't," said her daughter-in-law. "I've had all I can take. I give up."

"I'm going to phone Joshua. I might just catch him before he goes to work," said Tulip.

"You'll do no such thing," said Vinetta. "He's too far away to do anything. There's no point in worrying him."

"The phone's off anyway," said Pilbeam. "I tried to ring Albert. It's been off all day."

They lapsed into silence. Tulip sat in an armchair at the

other side of the sofa. She went on with her knitting. The clock on the wall ticked away two long hours.

Suddenly into the silent room came Wimpey, dressed in her nightgown, carrying her beloved American doll. She sidled up to Vinetta.

"I can't sleep," she said.

"Come beside me," said her mother holding out one arm. "We'll wait together."

"What are we waiting for?" asked Wimpey as she made herself comfortable by her mother's side.

"I'm not sure," said Vinetta. "We're just waiting."

Tulip gave Vinetta a stern look.

"It's not like the last time," she said. "That young madam knows what she's up to. She set off deliberately. It's my guess she's gone back to Brocklehurst Grove."

"And if she doesn't get there?" said Vinetta. "Anything could happen. Anything." She thought rapidly of all the disasters that could befall a rag doll on a motor scooter. It filled her with horror.

"Appleby can take care of herself," said Granny Tulip grimly, "probably better than you can, Vinetta. She'll come to no harm."

There was a thudding on the floor above, a vigorous, irritable thudding. Tulip sighed and went up to see Magnus. As she walked up the staircase she wondered if it might be possible to say nothing about Appleby's disappearance, to keep it a secret from the old man in the four-poster bed.

"Where's Appleby?" asked Magnus as soon as Tulip entered the room. "She's not gone off again, has she?"

"How did you know?" It was all Tulip could say.

"What do you think I am? Deaf or daft? Something's

going on down there and it involves Appleby. That I do know."

Tulip explained.

"So what do we do now?" she asked meekly.

Magnus patted her hand gently and gave her one of his wisest looks.

"We wait," he said. "It's all we can do. We should be used to it by now."

But, and he knew it, there are some things one can never get used to.

Wimpey was asleep, cradled in Vinetta's arms. Vinetta dozed. Pilbeam, still in the armchair, was tired but watchful. Minutes felt like hours. On the old sideboard, the clock ticked loudly.

When Tulip returned to the drawing-room which was lit now by only two table-lamps, the heavy curtains drawn against the night, she shook her head as she looked at her family.

"Bed," she said firmly and clearly so that they all looked up with a start. "There's no point in sitting here all night."

"I'm-Polly. What-are-you-called?" said the American doll as Wimpey accidentally pulled the string.

"Bed," said Tulip, holding out her hand to her sleepy little grandchild.

Pilbeam also stood up, stretching her arms above her head.

Vinetta sat upright on the sofa and looked stubborn.

"You must all go to bed," she said. "That makes sense. But I am staying down here. Someone might come to the door. The phone might ring."

"The phone's off," Tulip reminded her.

"No matter," said Vinetta. "Here I am and here I stay."

And she did. All the night long.

She did not know that Brocklehurst Grove had been saved. She did not know that Joshua was hugging his mug of cocoa and rejoicing. She did not know that Appleby had reached home safely. Fear was in possession of her soul and the waiting hours were full of imagined terrors.

31

Albert and Kate

At the end of Albert's Tuesday morning tutorial on Anglo-Saxon archaeology, Lorna Gladstone hung back, deliberately. Lorna, at the beginning of her second year, was now much more confident and less given to burbling. Her black hair was cut in a neat, long bob. Her eyes were almost as dark as Pilbeam's.

"Albert," she said when they were alone, "I hope you don't mind my asking you this, but does your family live in a place called Comus House?"

Albert stared wide-eyed at the girl and dropped the file with his notes on the Sutton Hoo ship burial so that papers scattered all over the floor.

Lorna stooped down, gathered up the papers into their folder and handed them back to her tutor with a kindly smile. Albert looked at her blankly. She reminded him of someone.

"I only asked," Lorna went on, "because my great-great-grandmother was a Pond. She lived at Comus House, out in the country near Allenbridge. My mother wondered if we might be distantly related."

"My great-grandfather was a Pond," said Albert, trying to get over his confusion.

"He would be," said Lorna, smiling.

Albert smiled back and felt more at ease. Lorna, he decided, looked and sounded a bit like Pilbeam. Quite a recommendation!

"Comus House belongs to me now," he said. "I'm going to have to sell it, of course, but I'll take you there some day when I get things organised a bit better. Perhaps your mother might like to come too."

Lorna looked at the clutter in the room and the jumble on his table.

"I won't hold my breath," she said.

"I know! I know!" said Albert. "But it is complicated."

More complicated than you could ever hope to guess, he thought, after Lorna had left. Their conversation had brought uncomfortably home to him how odd his life had become. He looked down at his desk and began to take his fountain pen to bits.

I should be leading a more normal life, he thought. I'm thirty-one years old. I could be married by now, raising a family. Yet all I think of is how soon can I get to Comus House, how much time can I spend there. I'm worried about Soobie and his depression. And that's just the latest worry! It's not natural. It cannot go on indefinitely.

"No, it can't," said a voice in the room, "and it won't."

Albert was startled. He looked up and there, sitting in the old fireside chair, was Aunt Kate.

"You can read my thoughts!" said Albert as shock gave way to surprise.

"It's not hard," said Kate. "You've sat there and dismantled a perfectly good fountain pen. It is not the action of an untroubled man."

Albert looked sheepish.

Strange the effect Kate had on things. The room felt isolated. The clock on the wall froze at ten past twelve, its sweeping red second pointer sticking just below the three.

"What do you mean when you say it won't go on? Have you thought of a way out for them?" Albert asked.

"No need," said Kate. "They've won. That's what I've come to tell you. Go to Brocklehurst Grove and see for yourself. Soon, very soon, you'll be able to bring my family home and once they're settled in again, you can go off and get on with your own life."

Albert took a while to grasp what she meant. Kate told him all about the banner and the broadcast and the descendant of Matthew James who belonged to the Establishment. Aunt Kate was a very knowledgeable ghost!

"So, you see, it will soon all be over," she concluded, "and won't they be pleased!"

She looked as if she were conferring a blessing when she told Albert that his services would no longer be needed.

Albert looked thoughtful, upset even.

"It's not as simple as that," he said. "I wish it were. I'd like everything to be nice and normal, but at the same time I don't want to forget them. I don't want to step out of their lives. They are my family now. All the family I have. I have learnt to love them. For as long as they want me, I'll be there."

Kate gave a deep sigh. Ghost though she was, the words chilled her. She gave Albert a look of pity.

"I am sorry. I am really, really sorry. I have been far too selfish. I have never given a thought to how this might affect you. There are things I know that I am not permitted to tell, but I know far less than you might think. Then there are powers I have that I am allowed to use, but, I tell you honestly, I am never quite sure what those powers are."

He looked at her. Suddenly she was not a tweedy, self-possessed elderly lady any more. Her outer appearance did not change, but Albert was aware of many selves occupying that shell — a lonely young girl, a child who was a tomboy up to all sorts of mischief.

"You once climbed up onto the roof," said Albert, seizing on a passing memory.

"Yes, I did," said Kate, smiling wistfully but regaining some of her composure. "That was when I was four. My father nearly had a fit!"

Albert felt muddled but aware of two odd facts. The ghost had her own history and she was all the people she had ever been. And, more important, the ghost might not have the power to solve the problems she had helped to create.

"I'll go to Brocklehurst Grove later this afternoon," he said firmly. "I'll see what's really happening and we'll take it from there."

Aunt Kate looked humble. It was a complete role-reversal. Albert was strong and decisive. Kate was weak and almost fearful. She got up from the fireside chair, wavered for a moment, and then faded into the blue of the door.

32

Tuesday — Appleby at Home

Appleby was stiff from sitting too long in the rocking-chair with her feet on the old footstool. A glance at her watch told her that it was one-thirty. The day was overcast and the attic was dreary. Appleby began to suffer the insufferable. She was totally bored.

The table had gone to the lounge downstairs, but the books were still there in a pile on the floor near the footstool. Appleby picked up *The Three Musketeers*, flicked through the pages and decided that the print was too small and the paper was too yellow. *Bleak House* she dismissed with a shudder, thinking of the bleak house she had just left. The other books she didn't even bother to handle. Clever she might be, but she was no reader. Magazines and paper-backed crime were all she could tolerate. It always seemed strange to her that Pilbeam and Soobie were so interested in books.

She looked at herself in the wood-framed mirror, tilting her chin and pouting her lips like a covergirl. Then she got bored with that and twisted her face into the most hideous expression she could manage.

"I'll go mad," she said explosively. "I'll die of boredom.

And I won't even be able to go downstairs tonight — he will be there."

She felt doubly irritated when she remembered that it was Tuesday night, Father's night off. So there would be no sneaking down after he'd gone to work.

She did not feel ready yet to explain her presence even to Joshua. There was always that pride about her that hated to be seen as being in the wrong. Had it been any other night but Tuesday she would have positively enjoyed snooping around the empty house.

She rummaged through the junk Soobie had once tidied away into a packing chest but, apart from a black lace scarf that looked as if it might come in useful some day, there was nothing worth having.

She opened the front of the doll's house and shut it again when she saw a large spider crouched inside surrounded by cobwebs and dust.

Then she rocked in the chair and dozed.

She awoke to hear noises from the room below. Joshua, waking from his daytime rest, was on his way downstairs again. It was three o'clock in the afternoon. All day he had hoped the telephone would ring, sleeping on Granpa's bed so as to be within reach of the handset. He had searched all of his pockets for the number Vinetta had written down. He had even looked under every clock and ornament. It was nowhere to be found. He was longing to speak to his wife and family. It was not exactly an 'emergency' but there was news that needed telling. Brocklehurst Grove was saved. The long loneliness was nearly over.

Appleby was irritated by the thought of her father sitting by the fire in the lounge, doing whatever he felt like doing, reading a newspaper or a magazine, even watching the television. It wasn't fair. She stuck it out for another hour. It grew dark and she tiptoed onto the landing and switched on the light. There was nothing for her to do. The television set was back in Soobie's room. Even the record player had gone. It was no use. No matter what her father might say or do, she could not stand the sheer boredom of the attic any longer.

So she went noisily down the attic stairs, ready to bluff it out. Serve him right if I give him a shock, she thought. All he thinks about is his job. Sydenhams, Sydenhams, Sydenhams!

Joshua, in the lounge with the door open in case the phone rang in the breakfast-room, had not thought about his job all day. He had thought about Vinetta and a house full of noise. So when Appleby clattered into the room, it came as no surprise.

"So you're back," he said. "Where are the others?"

It was Appleby who was shocked. She was used to her father's unflappability, but this surely must be the ultimate!

"I've just come down from the attic, Dad. I've been here since last night. Are you not surprised?"

Joshua drew on his pipe before speaking. It was a very useful pretend.

"What were you doing in the attic?" he asked, trying to focus on what she was saying.

Appleby gave him a look of exasperation.

"I was in the attic hiding from you. I've run away from Comus House. I borrowed Albert's scooter. It's in the garden shed."

Now it was Joshua's turn to look surprised.

"I thought Albert must've brought you. I thought you must all have found out," he said.

"Found out what, Dad? You can be very irritating at times, do you know that?" snapped Appleby.

"About the Grove being saved," said her father. "Did you not see the new banner?"

Appleby dashed to the bay window. There was a banner all right, out on the front street slung between Number 1 and Number 9. And it wasn't the same banner. This one was gold with blue lettering.

BROCKLEHURST GROVE IS SAVED
HIP! HIP! HOORAY!

She read the words with difficulty. They were a fair distance away. Their message faced the world outside and appeared to her as mirror-writing.

Appleby was overjoyed. She even gave her father a hug, which he had not expected, and being a very undemonstrative man, did not appreciate.

"Don't go wild," he said. "I knew what would happen, though I must say they've taken their time."

"Have you not rung Mum?" demanded Appleby. "They'll all want to know, and fast."

"I don't know the number," said Joshua. "Your mother wrote it down somewhere, but I can't find it. I've been waiting all day for a call."

"Do you never know anything? That number was one of the first things I learnt when we moved up there. I figured it might come in useful some day."

"So you phoned your mother as soon as you got here and told her you'd arrived safely," said Joshua, knowing perfectly well that she hadn't.

Appleby had the grace to look guilty, but she brushed guilt aside and said sharply, "Well, I'll ring her now. So that's all right."

But it wasn't all right. She dialled the number only to find that the line was completely dead.

"Bother!" she said. "Their phone's off. Nothing's ever right at that place."

Appleby flounced back into the lounge and flung herself full length onto the settee in front of the fire.

Joshua drew very hard on his pipe and didn't speak for some minutes.

"We'll just have to wait for Albert to come, then," he said at last. "He promised he'd be here some time today."

"Thanks for telling me!" said Appleby. "Getting any information out of you is like drawing teeth. If their phone hadn't been dead, you wouldn't have even mentioned Albert. You're useless."

If Appleby had spoken like that to any other member of the family there would have been a terrible row. But Appleby knew what to expect from her infuriatingly quiet father. He looked at her, shook his head, sighed a sigh of resignation and said nothing. It was not entirely unimpressive. Appleby looked back at him and felt ashamed. She didn't apologise. But she felt ashamed.

33

The Clouty Doll

On Tuesday morning, Vinetta awoke just before eight o'clock feeling dazed and not sure where she was or what was happening. She had stayed awake till five and then sleep had come unwanted and unbidden.

"Appleby," she said as she came fully awake. "Oh, Appleby! Why do you have to do such things?"

The clock on the wall did not answer and the dull heavy furniture that overcrowded the room was even more silent.

Vinetta rose stiffly from the sofa, switched off the light and opened the curtains. Outside, the day was at the grey stage which can hardly be described as day at all. The distant landscape slumbered under a blanket of mist.

Vinetta felt suddenly angry. It was not fair. She had done her best. She had always done her best. And now everything had fallen apart. Joshua was miles away, and oh how she missed the steadiness of his silence! Soobie was sulking. Appleby had disappeared. As for the rest of the family . . . here was a new day, it could be even worse than yesterday . . .

"Let's hope it's a better day today," said Tulip briskly as she came into the gloomy lounge. "A mistake to put the lights out this early. You can hardly see your hand in front of your face."

She switched on the light again. Vinetta automatically closed the curtains and went back to sit on the sofa. Tulip sat beside her and took both hands in hers.

"It *can* be better today, you know," she said. "As soon as the phone's back on we'll ring home. Appleby's probably there already. Remember, if we can't ring out, she can't ring in either."

"It's not just Appleby," said Vinetta. "It's Soobie too, and Poopie with his tantrums, and Hortensia hardly speaking. This place is a curse, Tulip."

"I've never heard such rubbish," said Tulip. "You sound like a silly, superstitious teenager. This place is a house. It doesn't suit us. We don't like it. But there it is."

It wasn't raining any more but the day stayed raw and dull. Soobie, of course, did not appear. Poopie also stayed in his room, the warrior sulking in his tent. Granpa slept all day. Tulip and Vinetta sat in the breakfast-room where Hortensia, after a lot of tactful persuading, joined them. They talked sporadically of old times and took turns nursing Googles. Pilbeam looked after Wimpey, played Snakes and Ladders with her half the day, and cards for the rest.

"Where do you think Appleby is?" asked Wimpey.

"She's at home in Brocklehurst Grove," said Pilbeam firmly as she threw the dice, "and soon we'll all be back there." She had no idea how true those words might turn out to be. It was a feigned optimism, meant to reassure Wimpey.

Pilbeam's throw landed her on a snake's head and she ended up back at square one. With all the superstition of an adolescent, she shivered.

"I'd have preferred to go up a ladder," she said.

"Well, I'm glad you didn't," said Wimpey, " 'cos I'm going to win."

No one bothered to open the curtains again at the front of the house that day. Only the library curtains were open, and that was because they were never shut.

So when Joe and Billy, playing detectives, came snooping around looking for clues early in the afternoon, the place looked genuinely deserted. The boys had chosen this way to spend a day's holiday from school. They left their mountain bikes carefully concealed in the hawthorn hedge. Using all their skills as commandos (learnt at the local Scout hut) they crept stealthily round the house, close to the walls, going in sharp bursts from one window to the next.

"Nothing here," said Joe in a loud whisper. "They must've got the stuff away in the night. Let's look for tyre marks."

They headed towards the drive on the north side of the house and came to the only window with its curtains open – the library. Cautiously raising their heads above the low sill, they peeped in.

"It's a clouty doll," said Billy in astonishment, "a bloomin' big blue clouty doll!"

And it was.

On the sofa that faced the window, stretched full length, was a life-sized cloth doll. Its hair was short-cropped and navy blue. Its face was a lighter blue and its eyes were silver buttons. Its blue-striped suit looked crumpled and dirty. Its blue leather slippers were clearly well-worn.

"I know what us could do wi' that," said Joe excitedly, forgetting all about his role as senior detective.

"Yeah!" said Billy, catching on more quickly than usual. "A guy for the bonfire. It'd be tremendous!"

"We'll ride down to the village and tell Geoff and Jimmy,

and the four of us can come back the night after dark and get it."

"Will we be able to get in the window, d'ye think?" asked Billy. He had no experience of breaking and entering. Smashing the window seemed a bit drastic. His dad would fell him if he found out. Jamie Maughan's rules were very, very strict.

Joe Dorward gave an expert look at the loose catch in the centre of the window.

"No problem there, Watson," he said, going back to playing detectives. "If our investigations take us into the house, entry through this window will be a cinch."

Soobie, wallowing in his own private misery, stared towards the window unseeing, and saw, and heard, nothing.

34

The Chase

It was six-thirty when Albert arrived at Brocklehurst Grove. He grinned broadly at Anthea's triumphant banner. It was delightful, if somewhat flamboyant, confirmation of what Kate had told him.

"Marvellous, isn't it?" he said when Joshua opened the door to him. "All we have to do now is fetch them all back home. I tried ringing them earlier on, but the phone's off."

Appleby had not gone to the door to welcome Albert. She had stayed discreetly in the lounge. She was brash and cheeky with the family and far from polite to Albert as a rule. But this was different. He would want to know what she was doing there and she did not want to be put on the spot when she was so obviously in the wrong. Her pride wouldn't suffer it.

"You tell him when he comes, Dad," she had said to Joshua in a wheedling voice. "Tell him how miserable I was at Comus House, and how brave it was of me to make my escape on the scooter."

Joshua hadn't said that, but he'd said enough.

"There she is," he said as he led Albert into the lounge. Appleby was sitting as upright as a queen in her high-backed

170

basket chair beside the round table. She looked at Albert defiantly.

"Well, I'm here," she said, "and it's a good job I am. It'll make one less for you to bring back. I managed on my own. Not one of them could."

Albert gave her an amused smile which was rather infuriating, but then made it better by going on to congratulate her on her part in saving Brocklehurst Grove.

"My part?" said Appleby.

"Yes. Remember, the petition was your idea. You started the ball rolling. If it had been left up to me, we would have just cut and run."

That was a master-stroke. Appleby, reinstated in her own eyes, said, "I don't know where they'd all be without me. They haven't a clue."

Albert rang the 'faults' number. For the third time that day he reported to the engineers the failure on the Comus House line.

"They won't get it on tonight," he said, "but another day won't make much difference. I only wish your mother knew you were safe, Appleby."

"Of course she knows I'm safe," said Appleby. "She's not stupid. And Granny will have guessed where I am anyway."

Albert still looked doubtful but contented himself with saying, "I have no lectures tomorrow morning. I'll dash up to Comus early on and let them know the news."

A peaceful night for Albert? Some hopes!

They were all going up to bed. It was only nine-thirty, but late enough considering all there was to be done the next day. Joshua was already in his room. Appleby was going up the second flight of stairs to hers.

"Goodnight, Appleby," Albert called. "I don't suppose I'll

see you in the morning. I'll go straight to Comus House. I'll have to set out at six, or maybe earlier."

"You'll go now," said a sharp voice behind him, a voice that only he heard.

Appleby's door had closed.

Albert turned and faced Kate. He knew the voice. What was worse, he knew the tone of voice. There she was, standing just a few yards from him, as solid and determined as ever. As a ghost, she was not in the least frightening. As a person, she was formidable.

"It's a dark, misty night," Albert protested feebly, "and I'm tired."

"Can't do anything about the weather," said Kate, "but I can take care of the tiredness. You'll have me beside you all the way."

"Why tonight?" asked Albert, falling into the usual trap of asking questions when a flat refusal would really have been the only way out.

"You'll see when we get there," said Kate, "but we're going to have to be very quick."

Before he knew what had hit him, he was in the Range Rover with Kate beside him and they were half-way out of Castledean.

"You'll have to drive faster than this," Kate protested, "or we'll never make it in time."

"I'm already doing forty-five," said Albert, law-abiding, careful Albert who never broke the rules, "and I should be doing no more than thirty."

"Faster," said Kate. "Put your foot to the floor."

"You must be joking," said Albert. "Have you any idea how fast this thing can go?"

"I would never ask you to do more than ninety," said Kate. "It would draw too much attention."

A startled Albert looked round at his passenger.

They had reached sixty.

"Keep your eyes on the road, Albert. Do you want to have an accident?"

The traffic lights ahead turned red.

"Drive straight through," said Kate. "We really haven't time to stop. The road's clear."

Albert, law-abiding, careful Albert who never broke the rules, drove straight through. His heart was in his stomach and goodness knows where his stomach was.

They made it to the country roads in one piece and without being arrested. Albert was almost relieved. True, the car was doing eighty-five along narrow, unlit roads, but at least there was no other traffic.

"The worst that can happen, I suppose, is that we'll land in a ditch," he said, feeling light-headed and strangely detached.

"Of course we won't. What do you think I'm here for?" Suddenly her voice became more urgent. "Sharp bend ahead. Road narrows. Car coming this way. Hold on to your hat."

It was not an expression Albert knew, but he understood the gist of it. As they neared the bend he managed to slow down to forty. His eyes misted over. The wheel then developed a will of its own and the Range Rover (thank heavens it was a Range Rover!) entered a ploughed field through one bit of hedge and exited through another. The innocent driver of the passing Fiesta was so far from believing his eyes that he convinced himself that he had never seen it.

They picked up speed again. It cannot be said that they were cruising at ninety. One cannot cruise at ninety along twisting roads in a Range Rover. Albert was terrified.

About twenty miles from Comus House came the crunch.

They had to join another road and shortly after the junction they came up behind an articulated lorry, heavy-laden, and doing a stately thirty-five.

"Pass it," ordered Kate. "For heaven's sake, pass it. We haven't got time to dawdle."

"I can't," said Albert. "I wouldn't dare. There could be something coming in the other direction. There isn't room. There could be one almighty accident."

"Will you stop worrying, Albert," said Kate furiously. "I know what's ahead for miles and miles. There are advantages to being what I am." She never, ever called herself a ghost.

But not even fear of Kate could make Albert pass that lorry.

"I can't. I won't. And I daren't," he said. "It's not just my own skin I'm worrying about. I could end up killing somebody."

"This is ridiculous," said Kate. "You should know by now that you can trust me. Close your eyes. I'll take over. Close them and keep them closed till I tell you to open them again."

Albert, careful, law-abiding Albert who never broke the rules, saw Kate's hand reach over to the steering wheel and he shut his eyes. He just couldn't bear to look.

"Do exactly what I tell you," said Kate, "and do it straight away."

The lorry was passed without disaster befalling them.

"Put your foot down a bit harder now," said Kate. "Give it all you've got. But don't open your eyes. I'm managing better without you."

She allowed him to ease off the accelerator for a sharp left turn, but then it was on again faster than ever.

The rest of the journey, all five minutes of it, passed without incident.

"You can slow down now," said Kate, "and open your eyes. Comus House is just round the next bend."

They turned sedately up into the drive that led to the stable-garage.

"Well?" said Albert tersely as he stopped the car and pulled on the handbrake. "What next?"

Kate was about to answer him when an instinct, stifled till now by the speed of their journey, made her suddenly aware of the terrible truth.

"We're too late, Albert," she said. "We're much too late!"

35

The Burglars

It was eight-thirty on Tuesday evening – the sky pitch black and the air damp and clinging. Four boys, two on bicycles, two trotting along holding the handles of a big barrow, came down the curving road towards Comus House. After putting the barrow and the bicycles into the shelter of the hawthorn hedge, the conspirators went stealthily up the track towards the house.

The younger Mennyms were all asleep. The women were still in the breakfast-room. The front of the house was in total darkness.

The first Soobie knew of danger was when two or three torches played their beams around the room and scanned the sofa where he lay. An instinct stronger than fear impelled him to stay absolutely still.

On the gravel path outside, the four adventurers stood and prepared to force an entry. It was something they had never done before. To them, this was an empty house, long forsaken, which had come strangely to life for a few short hours some weeks ago and then relapsed into its state of chronic disuse. It was not like breaking into somebody's home. And all they wanted was a guy for their bonfire. That was what Joe had argued. Billy was a bit unsure about this, but the rest were ready to agree with anything Joe said.

It was Joe who did the work. He put a long screwdriver in the join between the upper and lower window frames. The frames, being old, were loose-fitting. The clasp was rudimentary. Joe pushed it aside with very little effort.

"Hardest bit'll be raising the window," he said to his friends. "Them sashes can get stiff. They might even be broken."

"We'll manage it, Joe," said Geoff Martin, a fat, fair lad with powerful shoulders. "If we don't we'll just have to smash the glass."

"What about the noise?" said Billy Maughan. He was worried about his dad. He was dead worried!

"There's nobody here," said Jimmy Reed, a weasel of a lad with lank black hair and pale blue eyes. "There's nobody for miles. You could let a bomb off and nobody would hear it."

But, as it happened, there was no need to break the window. It opened with surprising ease and one by one the boys climbed over the sill.

"Look at it," said Joe, shining his torch on Soobie's impassive face. "Isn't it smashing? Can you just see it right on top of the bonfire on Tidy Hill?"

"Seems a shame to burn it, though," said Billy. "It's too good to burn." Soobie, hearing that, felt almost friendly towards him.

"Of course we'll burn it," said Joe. "Are you soft or something? That's what guys are for."

Soobie stayed limp. If the only way he could save his family from these marauders was to be burnt alive on their hideous bonfire, then so be it.

It is expedient for you that one man should die for the people . . .

The words came to Soobie's mind unbidden, a memory

of past reading, but in a moment he took them to his heart and resolved to save his people, no matter what the cost. If these intruders, whoever they were, should find out that the house was home to a whole family of living rag dolls, there would be no end to the misery it would cause. Soobie remembered only too sharply how his grandmother had called him a freak. All Mennyms are freaks, he thought. For what is a freak but someone or something outside the norm?

The boys dragged his limp body over the window ledge. Jimmy Reed gave a sudden howl.

"Dammit," he said. "I've caught me hand on a nail."

"Shut up, will you?" said Joe. "You're nothing but a big babby. There could easy be somebody in the house for all you know."

And there was, of course. There was a whole family of them. And they might have heard. Soobie was horrified at the thought. If they heard . . . if they came to see what the noise was all about . . . Even lights going on in the house would attract too much attention. Soobie was in agony. He lay on the grass like an old sack, becoming damper and dirtier as the boys looked dubiously up at the house. But it stayed unlit and silent.

Billy gave a suspicious glance at Joe. How could there 'easy' be somebody in the house when Joe had told them all it was empty? Joe was a good mate, but you could never be quite sure of him.

More quietly, the boys dragged the body over the damp grass. Billy held one torch to light the way. The others had put theirs away in their anorak pockets. Soobie was glad of the darkness and that the one beam of light was directed at the ground. They moved on towards the broad drive that led from the road to the stables.

Down they went to the hawthorn hedge and the bikes

and the barrow. Soobie was a head taller than Joe, and much broader. Had he been human, the task of putting him onto the barrow would have been even harder. Even so, it was awkward. Billy and Jimmy held onto the handles whilst Joe and Geoff wedged the guy into the narrower end of the barrow with his legs protruding either side of the long shafts.

"There," said Joe gasping, "that should do it."

Joe then grabbed one bicycle and Jimmy took the other.

"Geoff and you can push the barrow, Billy. Us'll help if it gets too hard," said Joe, "but we've got our own bikes to see to and it's not so easy uphill. Better if we'd all walked, I suppose. But it's a bit late to think about that now."

"I can push it easy," said Geoff. "I don't need little titch to help me. Out the way, Billy. I'll soon show you how to do it."

Geoff Martin was fair, fat, big . . . and dense as the proverbial forest. He spat on both hands and placed them in the centre of the barrow so that the two shaft handles were either side of him. Then with a great heave he set off at a run. Joe gave a smile that was not seen in the dark.

Geoff's pace soon slackened, but he did manage to push the barrow all the way to the Maughans' farmyard, which was where it had come from in the first place. All four boys helped manoeuvre the body up the fire escape into the loft. Once inside they switched on the light and admired their haul – one enormous, magnificent all-blue guy. Soobie's acting was brilliant. He lurched limply to one side of the chair in which they had sat him and looked as if he had never, ever known life.

But he watched the four guardedly, and he listened to what they had to say.

"Us'll keep 'im here till Thursday night. No good takin'

'im up the hill too soon. Somebody might nick him. There's some very dodgy characters about," said Joe.

"We can make on he's our prisoner," said Billy, "an' I can bring him bread and water."

Joe gave Billy a warning look. Trouble with Geoff and Jimmy was they had no imagination. They wouldn't understand about 'Holmes and Watson'. It was a game for only two players. Billy took the hint and said no more.

But when the other three went home, Billy went to Soobie and sat him upright on the chair.

"You are our prisoner," he said in a stilted, theatrical voice. "If you behave yourself, you will be treated well. But no trying to escape, mind you. No one has ever escaped from here."

Then he went out and came back with a black plastic tray on which he had placed a white enamel mug and a chipped tea plate.

"Here is your supper," he said. "I will return in the morning."

Then something about the clouty doll touched Billy's heart. The boy's grey eyes misted. This blue doll could be a friend of his. And they were going to burn him on Friday. Billy rested one hand on the doll's shoulder. Soobie felt a wave of sympathy and experienced a glimmer of hope. But the moment passed. The door shut and the boy locked it behind him.

Still, thought Soobie, it is only Tuesday. Friday is a long way off. Many things can happen before Friday.

36

Failure

"They've taken Soobie."

Aunt Kate stood helplessly beside Albert on the gravel path outside the library window. The Range Rover, parked at the top of the cart track, was their only illumination. But the open window was plain to see. The signs of a body being dragged across the grass were evidence enough. Added to this was Aunt Kate's psychic certainty that Soobie had been kidnapped.

"Children," she said. "Young children . . . but why?"

Albert said nothing. He was distressed and dazed. All that terrifying drive had been to no avail.

"Could you not have saved him without me?" he asked after a despairing silence.

Aunt Kate sighed and said, "There are things I'll have to explain to you, Albert. Come inside and sit down."

She stepped over the low window ledge, through the open window, into the library. A dazed Albert followed. They sat down, side by side, on the green plush sofa.

"Switch on the table-lamp," said Kate.

Albert did as he was told.

"I couldn't do that," said Kate. "I cannot do anything

physical, not even switch on a light. Without a human agent, I can do nothing. You are my agent, Albert Pond."

"I don't believe you," said Albert. "You steered the car, remember. You steered it past that lorry. I could not have done that."

"Your hands never left the steering wheel. If they had, I would have been helpless," said Kate. "What you experienced was pure hypnosis. I did know what was ahead in a way you could never have done, but it was you who controlled the wheel, not I. All I did was give you directions."

Albert still looked doubtful.

"If I reached my hand out to you now," said Kate, "and you attempted to grasp it, you would find that there was nothing but air between your fingers. I appear substantial enough, I know, but I have no substance."

Albert shivered.

"We'll not have a practical demonstration," said Kate. "I wouldn't want you to fear me."

Albert realised that he never had feared the ghostliness of Kate. She was a most unspectral spectre!

"You should have talked to Vinetta or Tulip. You should have warned them," he said. "That would have involved no more physical effort than talking to me. And it would have been much more effective."

"They have never seen me," said Kate. "They must never see me."

Albert was quick to understand. It was obviously up to him to rescue Soobie, wherever Soobie might be.

"You possess far more knowledge than I have," said Albert. "I may be able to save Soobie. But you are the only one who can find him."

"Limited," said Kate. "I cannot simply range the world. Within limits, I can be where you are. I can know what I am allowed to know. There is instinct, but that comes and goes as it will."

"Use your instincts now," said Albert. "Tell me where to find Soobie and I will rescue him myself."

"I can't," said Kate. "Instinct is a gift, but it cannot be summoned up at will. When the knowledge comes to me, I will find you, wherever you are, and guide you to Soobie. It will come. I have no doubt it will. We shall save him."

The room beyond the light of the lamp was all shadow. Kate stood up and faded away into the darkness. Albert was alone.

He switched off the lamp. Then he stepped over the sill again and went back to the car. Through the hours of the night he drove up and down country roads, hoping that Kate would reappear at his side to give him directions. But Wednesday's dawn came with no sign of doll or ghost. Albert returned to Comus House.

He let himself in the front door with his key. Vinetta was the only one astir. She had spent another restless night on the drawing-room sofa, wondering where Appleby had gone. When Albert came in, he hardly knew where to start. Vinetta rose to meet him.

"You had better sit down," he said. "There are so many things I need to tell you, and one of them is very, very serious."

"Appleby?" said Vinetta, startled.

"Appleby is safe at home in Brocklehurst Grove," said Albert. "So is Joshua. And the Grove has been saved. You will all be able to go home."

"Then," said Vinetta, looking puzzled, "what is it that is so serious? Why do you look so concerned?"

"It's Soobie," said Albert. "All we know, Aunt Kate and I, is that he has been taken away somewhere."

"Taken away? Who by? How? What do you mean?"

"Aunt Kate thinks he was stolen by a group of children, some sort of a game. That's all her instincts will tell her just yet. When she knows more she will come for me, wherever I am. Those were her words. We'll just have to trust her. I've searched the night for signs of Soobie's whereabouts, but he could be anywhere."

Vinetta was dumbfounded.

"Let's wake the others," she said. "Let's tell them."

"No," said Albert. "There really is nothing any one of us can do. Don't say a word to them unless you have to. They will think that Soobie is still in the library. And let's believe that by the end of the day that's where he will be. I've talked to Kate. I trust Kate. She will find him."

He did not add the words "if anyone can" and he felt uncomfortable when Vinetta said, "Are you sure?"

"As sure as I can be," he said. "When Aunt Kate knows his whereabouts, we will rescue him."

"But if these children, supposing it is children, know that Soobie is alive, what will they do?"

This was safer ground.

"Kate knows Soobie well enough," Albert said. "We all know Soobie well enough. It's a safe guess he will play dead till he is rescued, or can manage to escape. The situation is terrible. I won't try to make it seem less serious than it really is. But I honestly do believe that it is not desperate."

Then quite suddenly, as if a current had been switched off, Vinetta became calm. Her anguish had spent itself on Appleby. There was nothing left. But deep in her heart there was faith in Soobie, a rock-bottom confidence in his power to survive.

So Albert and Vinetta waited together in the drawing room, silently expecting Albert to receive some instant, supernatural summons. Tulip looked at them suspiciously when she came in. She sensed the strain.

They told her that Appleby was safe at home and that the threat against the Grove had been lifted.

"Then why do you both look so miserable?" asked Tulip with a sharp glance at each of them.

It was impossible to say nothing under such direct questioning. They told her everything.

When Miss Quigley appeared, she also had to be told the whole story. She listened, tight-lipped. Then, ignoring the others, she looked directly at Vinetta.

"He will be found, Vinetta," she said. "I know he will be found."

It was not instinct speaking, but a fierce determination not to believe the worst.

Poopic and Wimpey were told the good news but not the bad.

"When can we go home?" asked Wimpey.

"Soon," said her mother. "In a day or two maybe. Now go and play."

Pilbeam appeared just before eleven o'clock.

"Something's happened to Soobie," she said as she looked at their faces. "He's my twin. I know something has happened to him."

They told her the bad news along with the good. She looked at Albert.

"I trust you, Albert Pond," she said. "I only hope your confidence in Aunt Kate is well-founded. I wouldn't be as sure as you are that she can do what she promises."

Albert had a sudden lurching memory that he was supposed to be in Durham for two tutorials later that afternoon. If he set out straightaway he should just be able to make it. He explained his problem. He did not want to go, but to miss tutorials was in his eyes a cardinal sin. He already felt that Professor Hamilton was not entirely satisfied with his work.

"What if Kate wants you? What if she finds Soobie and needs you?" asked Pilbeam.

"Kate will come to me wherever I am," said Albert, "and I will leave whatever I am doing if I am needed. Once I am there, it won't be so difficult to make some excuse to leave if it becomes urgent."

Tulip supported his decision. "Nothing more can be done till Kate finds Soobie. Your work is your duty. Go and do it."

"I'll come straight back here as soon as I am finished," said Albert. "I should be back by seven-thirty – sooner if Kate calls me."

That afternoon Albert struggled through two tutorials with students who, from time to time, looked puzzled at his inattentiveness.

"Are you all right, Albert?" asked Lorna as she dawdled to gather up her books. Being distantly related made the question less impertinent.

"Yes, thank you," said Albert, smiling absently. "Late night, last night. That's all. Back to normal tomorrow."

But what was normal? Albert did not know any more. And who was to say what tomorrow would bring?

37

A Mennym and a Maughan

Early on Wednesday morning, Billy took Soobie his breakfast. A red plastic tray this time with a blue and white striped pint mug on it and a piece of cold toast on a tea plate.

"Had a good night?" he asked Soobie.

The doll in the old armchair gave not a sign. Dolls don't.

"Here's your breakfast," said Billy. "Tea's hot, mind. There's more toast if you want it."

Soobie sat still. It was hard not to give the boy a friendly look. Billy's eyes were dark-rimmed with lack of sleep. His wispy hair needed combing. He was weedy but wiry. What is more, it was evident to anyone who met him that he had a heart as big as a whale! A loving child of loving parents.

"Billy! Billy!" His mother's voice rang out in the farmyard. "Where've you got to this try? You'll miss that bus!"

Billy took one last look at Soobie.

The black tray with the tin mug and chipped plate was still on the box stool where he had left it the night before. The red tray was on top of an old packing case.

"I'll c'llect your dishes later," said Billy. He went out of the door and locked it behind him. Then he ran helter-skelter down the fire escape, his schoolbag bashing against the railings.

"There you are!" said his mother. "You spend too much time in that loft. I'll have to be giving it a sorting. Goodness knows what kind of mess you've got up there."

She smoothed his hair down with her hands and looked critically at his face. Billy looked back anxiously.

"There's no mess, Mam," he said. "Honest there's not. You said it could be my place. It's tidy as anything. Promise you won't go in. Promise."

Molly Maughan looked down at his earnest little face and laughed. For her, it was the most lovable face in the world, but laughing was easier.

"Won't have time today anyway," she said. "So I can safely promise to stay out. But I'll be up there on Saturday. Don't say you haven't been warned!"

Billy gave a sigh of relief. Saturday was fine with him. The doll would be gone by then.

On the bus to school he sat next to Jimmy Reed. Remembering the warning look Joe had given him, Billy did not talk about taking meals to the prisoner. It was Jimmy who first mentioned the guy.

"Got the you-know-what safely locked away?" he asked with a sly look over his shoulder to make sure no one was listening.

"Yeah," said Billy. "No problem."

Geoff and Joe went to the senior school, so they didn't meet up at all during the day.

At tea-time Billy was itching to go back up to the loft, but he stayed resolutely casual in case his mother should suspect anything. Joe was coming over later but by then his mother would be dividing her time between the dishes and the TV. Billy's dad did not like Joe, but his mother was pleased that her son had a friend to play with in the long winter evenings.

"That lad's mother shouldn't let him roam the countryside," Jamie Maughan would say.

"That's her business," was Molly's standard reply. "As long as our Billy's not roaming the countryside, that's all we have to worry about."

Which was why the loft was made available. It kept Billy safely at home.

It was seven o'clock before Billy decided to go up to the loft.

"Joe's coming over for an hour or so," he said to his mother. "I'd best be there for him coming."

Joe would not be coming till nine o'clock – but that was something Molly was never told. Many's the time Joe was left hiding in the loft whilst Billy went noisily to bed only to sneak out again later. Joe was a good teacher in guile and Billy was a willing learner.

Billy deliberately dawdled across the yard and up the fire escape. He was longing to run but running might look suspicious. That was another thing Joe had taught him.

"I've come to c'llect the dishes," said Billy to Soobie as soon as he had got into the loft and switched the light on. He put the red tray on top of the black one, together with both mugs and both plates.

"You didn't eat the toast," he said. "Waste of good food. Don't blame me if you're hungry."

He put the trays on the floor and sat himself down on the box stool.

"You will be transferred to the County Gaol tomorrow," he said to Soobie, looking earnestly up at the blue face and the desperately passive silver button eyes. "Treason in wartime is punishable by death."

Billy had just made up his mind that there would have to be a war on in this game and that Soobie must be Carlos, an enemy agent.

Then suddenly reality came in like a cold wind. The blue doll was really going to meet his end. He was going to burn on the bonfire on Tidy Hill. Billy looked at him and faltered. Soobie's face had an expression that was kindly and innocent.

"You didn't do it," said Billy vehemently. "I know you didn't. You are going to be shot at dawn and you are an innocent man. I will help you to escape. Stay here for now. Remain absolutely silent."

Billy took the trays down the fire escape. He left the loft door wide open. If Soobie had wanted to run he could have done so there and then. But he decided to wait. There might be a safer, surer way.

Billy sneaked into the kitchen with the trays and made sure that his parents were safely in front of the set. They were watching *Coronation Street*. Billy knew that they would be channel-hopping to find something else after that finished.

"I'm away to bed now, Mam," he called.

"Goodnight. I'll bring you a cup of chocolate later."

"No need. I'm dog tired. I'll be going straight to sleep."

"Joe not come?"

"No. He mustn't be bothering."

Billy went to his room and arranged his bed to look as if someone were sleeping in it. He left the door slightly ajar. His mother would not come right in. When he was younger she had always tucked him up at night. But not any more! The last time she had come in and kissed him gently on the cheek he had woken up with a start and shouted at her for being soppy. It saddened her, but she understood that he was becoming too grown-up to be babied.

Feeling safe from discovery, Billy went and fetched the

barrow from the corner near the hen house. He was too small to grasp both handles at once, but remembering Geoff's method he got between the shafts and grasped the middle strut of the barrow itself. He pushed it to the bottom of the fire escape.

The next job was to get the doll down from the loft. No easy task. Soobie offered as little resistance as he possibly could without rousing suspicion. On the iron rungs of the fire escape he managed, imperceptibly, to cheat a little. Billy felt quite proud of himself when he finally had the doll wedged in the barrow.

"Now, Carlos," he said to Soobie, "we must be very quiet. I am taking you to a safe house. You can remain there till the heat is off."

And by the heat he meant not only the heat of the bonfire but his mother's threatened Saturday visit to the loft. Billy figured out that he might really be able to keep Carlos once the weekend was over. All he had to do was to make sure that the others didn't find him before Friday. After that, he and Joe could play with him. They could make him one of their team. Joe might be mad before the bonfire. It would be necessary to tell him a few lies. But when it was over he would come round. Then he would be glad that Billy had saved the doll.

Going carefully in the darkness, Billy pushed the barrow through the big double gate and stopped to close it behind him. The only safe place he could think of was a ruined cottage two miles away, just before the junction with the road that led round and down to Comus House. Further up that road was the petrol station, the only one for miles around, and further on again in that direction the road dipped down into a valley before coming to Tidy Hill. Distances much more easily covered on mountain bikes! But for now, Billy had the barrow and was taking it down a gentle slope just as far as the ruins. Only the fragments of two walls were left standing, but they formed a corner and that is where Billy planned to hide his friend.

"What you doin' wi' that!" Joe Dorward shouted.

Billy had not heard him coming. He nearly jumped out of his skin.

"Nothing," he yelled. "None o' your business."

Joe had been on his way to see Billy. He had expected to find him at home guarding the prisoner. So what was he doing out here struggling with the barrow and the big blue clouty doll?

"What you doin'?" Joe insisted, grabbing Billy by the arm and threatening to twist it.

"Leave go," said Billy. "Give over and I'll tell you what I'm doin'."

"Right. Tell. And make it quick," said Joe.

"I'm hidin' Carlos from me mam. She's goin' to clear the loft and if she finds him she'll want to know where I got 'im from. You know what she's like."

It was a plausible explanation.

"Now you've got the barrow this far," said Joe, "I suppose we might as well push it the rest o' the way to Tidy Hill."

Billy said, tentatively, "Are you sure you want to put 'im on the bonfire?"

"Course I'm sure," said Joe. "What else could you do with 'im?"

"We could call him Carlos," said Billy eagerly. "And he could be a double agent working for our side against the enemy. And we could have drop-offs and secret codes and all sorts."

Joe was tempted, but only for a moment.

"We couldn't do that even if we wanted to," he said.

"Geoff and Jimmy would be livid if we didn't put it on the bonfire. It's their guy as well as ours. An' if you told them about our game they'd laugh themselves silly. Anyhow, it's a smashing guy. Most guys look nothing when they're right on top of the bonfire. That one's big enough to look the real thing."

In the darkness, Billy's lips twitched. It was all he could do to stop himself crying.

"I was goin' to dress 'im in me cousin Stan's old tracksuit. It's blue with white stripes and it would've fit him perfect."

"Pack it in," said Joe. "It's a bundle of old rags we're talking about, you know. That's all."

So saying, he lifted one handle of the barrow.

"Come on," he said. "Gi's a hand. You take the other handle and we'll do a steady trot."

"It's too late to go all the way to Tidy Hill," said Billy making one last ditch attempt to save the doll.

"Why, no it's not," said Joe. "It's not even half past eight yet. We can be there and back afore ten."

Billy could do no more.

Soobie suddenly saw how it would be. He could have escaped when the loft door was left open. But he had waited for a better opportunity. If Billy had left him at the cottage he could have been gone in the night and nobody any the wiser. They would have thought that someone had come along and stolen him. Now, it would become more and more difficult to be sure of getting away. His earlier resolution, to burn rather than be found out for what he really was, had had time to weaken. Martyrdom needs a strong and urgent cause. Comus House was far enough away by now, and his very absence would have warned the others of danger.

The boys were pushing the barrow uphill. They passed the petrol station. Soobie recognised it and remembered clearly the way back to Comus House. Then he made up his mind what he must do.

Soobie looked from one boy to the other. With the movement of the barrow they did not notice the turning of his head. Darkness hid the gleam in his eye. How to escape needed some seconds of thought. He was lying back in the barrow, facing the two boys. As the hill grew steeper, they bent lower over the shafts they held, so that Soobie saw only the tops of their heads. If he sprang forward suddenly, he would be able to run out between them. He gathered himself for the effort. He leapt. And he ran!

The boys let go of the barrow and screamed in terror.

"It's haunted," yelled Billy.

"It's a devil," shouted Joe.

They stared after the retreating figure. Yells turned to silent gasps.

Then Soobie tripped up and fell.

"He's fallen," said Joe. Devils don't fall and ghosts don't fall.

"It's a robot," said Joe. "There must be something inside it making it go. Maybe the jogging of the barrow set it away. Come on, we'll get it."

The barrow was lying on its side. They righted it and went pell mell down the hill towards the robot. Soobie startled them by getting to his feet.

"Wow!" said Joe. "Some robot that is! We've got to catch him now. Mebbe he's programmed to go back to that house. Hurry!"

Soobie heard the barrow bumping down behind him. With all the strength he could muster he ran towards the petrol station. Once past that lit-up landmark he would be on home ground. He could dodge and weave and hide out till morning if need be. Those boys had mothers too, just like Vinetta. They would hardly dare stay out the whole night long.

Then, with a spasm of terror, he realised that they were gaining on him. He had left his run too late! He had nearly reached the long, low boundary wall of the garage forecourt. In seconds the chase would be over. He would be caught before he could find a place to hide.

38

Albert's Marathon

By the time the tutorials were over, Albert was exhausted. There had been no supernatural call. His heart was weighed down with sadness. His body was being tested beyond endurance. It was Wednesday tea-time. He had not slept or even lain in a bed since Monday.

He went home to Calder Park. It was like entering a haven of peace. No students. No Mennyms. And, for now at least, no Kate. Compared to Comus House or even Brocklehurst Grove, this was toy town. Everywhere was tiny — two up, two down and a kitchen-dinette. Everywhere was clean and tidy — thanks to Mrs Briggs. Albert made himself a pot of coffee. He dozed in the chair by the living-flame gas fire for half an hour. Then he pulled himself awake with a jerk. It would have been heaven just to go on sleeping. But duty called. After another cup of coffee, Albert went out to the Range Rover and set off for Comus House. He turned the window down to let in the cold air. He switched on the radio. When this is all over, he said to himself, I will sleep the clock around.

The clock on the dashboard told him that he would not reach Comus House at the promised time. Still, an hour late was not too bad. Kate had not called him yet. That was the main thing.

When he reached Comus House, he saw that he was running very low on fuel. So he did not turn into the drive but drove straight on.

I'd better go up the road to the petrol station, he thought. Safer to fill up in good time, just in case I need to set off in a hurry. Tired though he was he felt compelled to go the extra mile. Or two. Or three.

It was when he was in sight of the petrol station that he realised fully why he had felt so compelled to go there. He looked ahead and there, running down the road in his direction, he saw Soobie. Behind him, coming out of the darkness, gaining on him, were two boys pushing a large barrow. Albert put on a bit of speed and, coming level with Soobie, he pressed hard on the horn, slowed the car to a walking pace, flung open the door of the passenger seat and hauled his friend in beside him.

"Close thing," he said to Soobie as he took a right turn into the garage forecourt.

Billy and Joe stood stock still for a few seconds and watched open-mouthed as Albert got out of the car and began to fill the tank. The boys were at the low boundary wall. The barrow was beside them, nose down to the ground. Joe was the first to recover. He raced across the forecourt and yelled at Albert, "That's our guy you've got there, mister. Who do you think you are?"

"I am Frankenstein," snapped Albert, "and that is my monster. Now scram, the pair of you."

Albert gave a rueful, apologetic glance across at Soobie, but the sensitive blue Mennym had not heard.

Billy came up alongside Joe. He looked expectantly at his

older, wiser, braver friend. Joe was nonplussed. It was Billy who spoke first.

"We don't believe you, mister. You're a rotten liar. That's Carlos and he belongs to us."

Albert looked down at Billy's indignant face. It was hard to take him seriously, especially as he stood there calling Soobie 'Carlos'.

"Listen, son," said Albert. "You could be in serious trouble for all you've done. Think yourself lucky I'm not calling the police."

At the word 'police', Joe began to look wary. One more word from Albert and they would both have run off, but Albert lost the initiative when he turned his back on them and concentrated on the petrol pump. The two boys stood sullenly watching.

"Let's go," said Billy.

"And let him think he's scared us?" said Joe. "Us'll go when we're good and ready. Not afore."

Albert finished filling the tank and hurried towards the kiosk to pay the bill. The garage had a very spacious forecourt. It was a good few yards from the pumps to the kiosk. Soobie, sitting in the passenger seat, began to feel worried. The boys eyed Albert's back thoughtfully and Soobie knew exactly what they were thinking. A quick grab, a fast retreat, find some bushes to hide in . . . They came at the car in a rush.

"Give over," yelled Soobie as they reached towards him. "Lay one finger on me and I'll crush your bones."

The boys ran. They didn't even retrieve the barrow. To see the 'robot' run, and to explain that away as some inner mechanism, was one thing. To hear him talk, and utter such threats, was quite another.

When Albert turned round again, the boys were nowhere

in sight. He got back in the car and drove off in the direction of Comus House. His brush with the kidnappers seemed to him something of a joke now, especially when Soobie explained how they had run away. Albert laughed out loud. But Soobie was worried.

"I don't think we'll have heard the last of them," he said. "When they have got over the shock they'll start nosing around. They might even tell people about us. Comus House won't be safe any more."

"No one will believe them," said Albert. "Their parents probably don't even know that they are out. Besides – Comus House won't need to be safe much longer. You will all be returning to Brocklehurst Grove."

He told Soobie the good news in some detail, but Soobie hardly listened. Only one thing mattered – to go home again to the only place where he felt that he truly belonged.

When they reached Comus House it was all lit up. Vinetta and Tulip were at the front door, watching for the car. Albert was late.

"Albert is always late," said Tulip. "When have you ever known him to be early?"

"Kate might have called him," said Vinetta. "He might be bringing Soobie home."

And, of course, he was. They spotted the headlamps of the car as it turned up towards the house and they rushed out to meet it.

Vinetta felt a surge of joy when she saw her son in the passenger seat. The car stopped and Soobie jumped down and ran to his mother. She hugged him and hugged him again. Then she looked at his dirty face and his ragged blue striped suit.

"That'll never mend, Soobie," she said. "I'll have to make

you another one. There's a whole roll of that material back home."

Soobie gave a sidelong look at his grandmother before speaking.

"I don't think I'll have another striped suit," he said. "I would prefer a dark blue tracksuit with white bands round the cuffs. You can get me one at Castledean Market."

Vinetta was surprised, but very pleased.

"I'll get a light blue one too," she said, "to change with it."

That, however, was going *too* far!

"No," said Soobie. "One dark blue tracksuit. That's all I need."

Albert put the car away. Then they all went into the house. It was ten o'clock. The young ones were in bed. The rest of the family fussed over Soobie. Albert sat in an armchair by the fire and fell asleep.

"Albert's asleep," said Pilbeam.

"Albert. Albert," said Tulip. "You should be in bed. Go up now, straightaway. What time would you like to be called in the morning?"

"Seven o'clock will be soon enough," said Albert. "I will go to bed now. I am desperately tired. Goodnight, everybody."

39

Holmes and Watson

Billy was crying, but his friend did not scoff him. Joe Dorward might be a schemer, a liar and a bit of a thief, but when it really mattered he was on the side of the angels.

"I'm scared," said Billy.

"I know," said Joe. "But they're gone now, whoever they are. We're safe, Billy."

Billy gave him a wild look, the wispy hair really was standing on end.

"But it was terrifying, Joe. It was really terrifying."

He began to cry again.

Joe felt sympathetic but uncomfortable.

"I was there an' all, y'know," he said. "It *was* terrifying. But it's over. Like I'm telling you – they're gone."

"Whereabouts did they go?" asked Billy, rubbing his eyes with his sleeve.

"Toward Comus," said Joe. "That's where they'll be goin'. That's where it came from, remember."

Billy was staring down the road and thinking.

"I talked to it," he said. "I was in the same room with it. I took it some supper and some breakfast – make-believe like. It was just a rag doll – a dummy. It never give the least sign of bein' live. It's been a night 'n a day in our loft. It knows where I live. What if it comes back?"

Joe thought about that one.

"It won't, man. It just wanted to get away. I don't know what to make of it any more than you do, but it won't be looking for you, that's for sure."

"I liked it. It had a nice, friendly face," said Billy, still trying to grasp it all.

Then Joe suddenly saw everything quite clear.

"It was computerised!" he said. "Why didn't I think of that before?"

Billy looked at him uncertainly.

"Simple," he went on. "Words and all. There must be a microchip inside it somewhere."

"But computers can't just say anything, like people do," said Billy. "When we went to get him, he told us to give over and he said he'd crush our bones."

"Recorded message," said Joe, "to warn people off – like me dad's car alarm."

Then he went on to be positively brilliant.

"It didn't come on when we took it from Comus House. It must be activated somehow. That fella in the car must have a remote control. That would even explain how the doll jumped out of the barrow in the first place. The man was searching for it and he must've come within radio range just at that moment. Don't you see, Watson? That man's a scientist. Goodness knows what he's up to. This calls for a real investigation."

Billy cheered up. The shock was beginning to wear off anyway. Joe's explanation sounded totally convincing.

"Yes, Holmes," he said, joining in the game, "we'll spy out the land on Saturday and see what is really happening in Comus House."

"No," said Joe. "That's too long to wait. He'll know we've rumbled him. He'll be gone by then. He looks a slippery character to me. Tomorrow. We'll check that place out tomorrow."

"I can't," said Billy. "Me cousin Stan's coming tomorrow tea-time. They'll expect me to be there."

"I was thinking of tomorrow morning, Watson," said Joe, looking sly.

"Us'll be at school," said Billy.

"We could stop off, you know," said Joe, introducing his innocent friend to the idea of playing truant. Billy had never missed school without his mother knowing. The school bus took him to school. The school bus brought him home. It was very rare that he missed the bus. If he did, either his dad took him, or his mam took him in later in the morning and apologised for his lateness. It needed a lot of persuasion to get him to realise that he could miss the bus 'accidentally on purpose' and not go back to the house and tell his mam. But finally it was agreed. They would both leave home as if for school and they would meet at the ruined cottage. Hardest part would be sneaking their bikes out, but it could be managed.

"And I'll bring me dad's binoculars," said Joe. "They're better than the ones you've got. If you could bring some biscuits or something that would be a help. It might be a long stint."

Then they got up from the rough grass where they had been sitting. The petrol station and the barrow were in full view. Not a soul in sight, fortunately. Billy was still a bit shivery as they went down to retrieve the barrow. Joe looked at his frightened face and understood.

"I'll come home with you," he said.

"Are you sure? Will your mam not miss you?"

"She'll be too busy serving the regulars. It's not even ten o'clock yet."

They reached the farm and put the barrow away.

"Thanks, Joe," said Billy.

"What for?"

"For coming all the way home with me. I'd have been scared on me own."

"Well," said Joe, proudly conscious of being twelve, "I'm a lot older than you, Billy. When you get older, it's easier not to be scared. See you tomorrow."

Joe and Billy reached Comus House just after ten o'clock on Thursday morning. The weather was cold and crisp. The fears of the night before seemed unreal in the brightness of the day.

There was a rough stone wall stretching the length of the vegetable garden on the north side of the cart track. It formed a boundary to the Comus grounds. It was very old, probably older than the house, and uneven. Bits of it were five or six feet high. Then it would dip down, saddle-like, to a height of no more than three feet. The boys chose one of the dips as a vantage point. At first they took care not to be seen, but as the house seemed dead they soon gave up all caution. They leant on the wall, took turns with the binoculars, and shared a snack of fig rolls and chocolate ginger snaps.

"Best I could do," said Billy.

"Good enough," said Joe.

For over an hour nothing happened in or around the house. The curtains that had been open when they arrived were still open. The curtains that had been closed were still closed. The boys were well wrapped up against the cold. Joe had even thought to bring a flask of tea. It was playing truant and having a picnic and it should have been good fun. But after an hour had passed it became boring.

"I think they must've gone, Holmes," said Billy. "Skipped in the night."

Joe yawned, but said firmly, "These long watches can get very tedious, but it is important not to give up too soon."

He handed the binoculars to Billy.

Just at that moment the front door opened. Wimpey came out with her skipping-rope.

"There's somebody there," said Joe urgently. "What can you see, Watson?"

Billy focussed the binoculars and looked towards the front door. On the path in front of it was a little girl skipping. He could plainly see her mittened hands turning the rope, her bunches of golden curls bobbing up and down. Then, looking carefully at her face, he saw something he could not believe.

"It's another one," he yelled, and Joe slapped one hand over his mouth.

"Be quiet," he said in a loud whisper. "She'll hear you."

They ducked down behind the wall.

"But, Joe," said Billy, "it's not a girl, not a real girl. It's another rag doll."

Joe grabbed the binoculars. He couldn't be totally sure. The girl was in the shadow of the house. But then she skipped along the path in their direction. As she grew closer Joe was able to see that Billy was absolutely right.

"It must be a research lab," said Joe. "They must be making them here. I wonder what for? This could be something big, Watson, something really big."

"I think we should go home, Joe," said Billy. "We might get into a lot of trouble."

"Go home now?" said Joe. "And miss out on all of this? You must be joking."

Joe went on staring through the binoculars.

The front door opened again. No one else appeared but a voice called, "Wimpey! Wimpey! Come in here this minute."

For what felt like eternity, nothing else happened. Billy and Joe took one short break. They cycled down to a village south-west of Comus House, built along a single main street that looped up off the road and then down again. Joe went into a little general dealer's store and bought two cans of Pepsi. Then they pedalled back to their vantage point.

"Hope we haven't missed anything," said Joe.

Billy yawned. This was much more tiring than going to school. School!

"Us'll have to be home afore four o'clock, Joe, or there'll be murder on!"

Joe looked at his watch.

"It's only ten past three. We can watch another twenty minutes, surely."

Just as they were finally about to leave, their patience was rewarded. A green car came up the cart track. It passed so close that they could see the driver's face and they recognised their enemy of the night before.

Joe thumbed his nose at him. Billy stuck his tongue out. Albert did not see these gestures, of course. He was looking towards the house.

"We'll have to go now," said Billy.

"O.K." said Joe. "Don't get in a flap. We're going. But let's come back tonight. I mean late tonight, after your mam thinks you're safe in bed. Bring your sleeping bag and something to eat . . ."

Albert had done a full day's work – three morning lectures

and an afternoon tutorial. Then he had made a beeline for Comus House. Arrangements would have to be made for bringing the Mennyms home.

When he arrived, he found everyone bursting to tell him the news. For whilst Billy and Joe had been outside, training the binoculars on the house, the Mennyms had been only too aware of their presence.

Soobie had spotted them first as he looked from the library window. Beyond the garage, on the wall that made a drunken boundary to the vegetable garden, he saw light reflected off the binoculars. Then he saw movement. He ran off to tell the others that there were strangers outside watching them. It was only after Pilbeam had brought the yellow binoculars from Appleby's room that they were able to identify the spies outside. Wimpey was the last to know of this new peril, which was why she had gone out so blithely with her skipping-rope.

Poopie rushed to get his word in first, especially the bit about Wimpey. Albert had barely closed the door behind him before the news was broken. No one even got the chance to say hello.

"There's two boys out there watching us through binoculars," said Poopie, "and Wimpey went out in the path, and they saw her."

"They're the same ones who took me away," added Soobie.

"We'll have to get out of here, Albert," said Vinetta. "We'll all have to leave tonight. They might bring a whole gang and break into the house."

Tulip was in less of a panic, but she agreed.

"It would be a shame if anything went wrong now that we are so near success. It's really just a matter of doing more quickly something we were going to do in any case. I've explained it to Magnus. He is getting dressed."

Albert looked at her wonderingly. Take *all* of them back in one night?

"It's not a minibus, you know, Tulip," he said. "It'll take more than one trip."

"That's why we should set off as soon as people are ready," she said.

Albert groaned, but agreed.

40

Home

It took all Thursday evening and into the early hours of Friday morning to move the whole of the Mennym family back to Brocklehurst Grove. Albert conveyed them there in three round trips. Albert, careful, law-abiding Albert, refused to carry more passengers than there were seat belts. And he kept within the speed limits. On each of the three journeys, every available luggage space was filled up with cases, boxes and bags. Each time they arrived at Brocklehurst Grove, Albert's return to Comus was slowed down by the necessity of unloading.

On the first trip he took Pilbeam, Miss Quigley and Googles. The baby, in her carrycot, was secured safely in the back seat. Miss Quigley sat beside her, very stiff and very upright. She kept both eyes on the road ahead. Most of the time there was nothing to see but headlights piercing the darkness of winding country roads. It was a relief when they came to the outskirts of Castledean. It was heaven when they reached Brocklehurst Grove.

"Just leave everything in the drive, Albert," said Pilbeam. "We'll manage to take them into the house after you go."

By the time Appleby came down, Albert had already

driven away. Appleby looked at Pilbeam, unsure of what her sister might say about the scooter escapade. But Pilbeam just shook her head and said briskly, "Well, don't just stand there. We have work to do."

The passengers on the second journey were Vinetta, Poopie and Wimpey. Wimpey slept the whole way, but Poopie was wakeful and miserable. He had grown to love Comus House, especially the yard and the stable. And he had not given up hopes that Andy Black might return.

"He'll wonder where I've gone," he said to Vinetta.

She looked over her shoulder at her unhappy little son and said, "He'll have found his own family now. They've probably been looking for him."

When they came to Brocklehurst Grove there was another unloading. Appleby took one look at Vinetta and, in a once-in-a-lifetime demonstration of affection, hugged her mother and said very, very quietly, "I'm sorry, Mum." Without a word, Vinetta returned the hug.

Joe and Billy returned to their posts just before midnight. Soobie, waiting in the doorway of the house, looked towards the wall and caught a glimpse of torchlight, no more than a glimpse. As soon as the boys had settled themselves comfortably behind the wall, they put out the torches. But the glimpse was enough to make Soobie suspicious. He felt sure they were being watched again.

The car drew up in front of the house ready to make the third trip. "That car's come back," said Joe. "Ready to work under the cover of darkness."

"But us are here watching," said Billy. "Us'll see whatever they're up to."

"There's dirty business going on over there," said Joe in his detective voice. "It could even be — murder!"

Billy shivered and hoped that Joe was wrong. It was very hard to go on playing a game when fact and fiction became so mixed up. People were coming out of the house. Harmless-looking people — an elderly woman and an old man with a stick. Not real villains, thought Billy with some relief. It could still be fun. It could still be just a game.

Tulip sat in the front passenger seat. It was decided that, even in the silence and the darkness of the night, it would be safer if Sir Magnus and Soobie travelled in the back.

Soobie was the last to come out of the house. The light behind him turned him into a bulky silhouette. He looked over to the wall where the spies had been all day, and had probably returned to watch again. He thought of Billy with his wizened little face, his warmth and his bravery. It would be like him to sneak away from home and be a watcher in the night. Safety was near enough for Soobie to take a risk. He turned towards the wall and, raising his right arm high in the air, gave a slow, curving wave.

"It's the clouty doll," whispered Billy. "It's Carlos. He's waving at us!"

Joe grabbed him by the hem of his coat to hold him back or he would have run down to the car.

"Where the devil do you think you're going?" he asked in as loud a whisper as he dared.

The two boys crouched down behind the wall. The blackness of the night enveloped them. And in that moment they were two very frightened children who had seen they knew not what.

"It wasn't a robot," whispered Billy, clutching Joe's arm.

Joe shivered. He too was suddenly and inexplicably sure that, whatever it was, the blue creature was not a robot. Terror seized him. "Run," he said. "Don't talk. Don't think."

They scrambled down the hillside to their bikes, dragging

their sleeping bags along the ground behind them. With fumbling speed, they prepared to mount. Then they pedalled frantically uphill towards the safety of home.

"Ride as fast as you can," said Joe. "And don't look back."

A chilling breeze began to blow. It was as if the spirit of the place was laughing at them as they had their turn to feel a spasm of terror.

"The darkest hour is just before the dawn," said Magnus as he alighted stiffly, helped by Soobie and Albert. The latter gave a groan as he thought how little time was left for sleeping.

The hall was full of luggage. The house was not its usual tidy self. But how marvellous it was to be home! They all saw Number 5 Brocklehurst Grove as they had never seen it before. Things familiar seemed strange and beautiful.

"You'll stay till morning, of course," said Tulip to Albert as they sat down in the lounge. "I'll make you a pot of tea. And there are still some real biscuits in the biscuit barrel."

"I think I'll just go straight to bed if you don't mind," said Albert. "I have to go to work tomorrow."

They helped Sir Magnus up to his own bedroom. Then Albert went to the guest room on the floor below (Soobie's room really) and as soon as his head touched the pillow he went out like a light. His first lecture in the morning was at eleven o'clock, a lecture fortunately and not a tutorial. He would stand behind his desk and deliver his thoughts on Charlemagne as he had done year after year for the past five years. He had begun to think that there were some lectures he could do in his sleep. This might have to be one of them!

41

Friday

Vinetta looked round the kitchen: her own sink, her own cooker, her own table and chairs. The warmth of their familiarity enfolded her. The twin-tub was less endearing. She remembered regretfully the automatic left behind at Comus House. Still, she thought, one can't expect to have everything.

The clock on the wall said five-thirty. Tulip came in.

"Have you not been to bed yet either?"

"No," said Vinetta. "I felt too wound up. I wanted to get used to being home."

"I know what you mean," said Tulip. "I've sat in the breakfast-room sorting out papers for the past hour, though I know it would make more sense to leave it till morning."

"Joshua will be pleased we're back," said Vinetta.

Tulip gave a short laugh.

"He'll probably forget we've ever been away. You'll see! He'll come in and find us all here. He might mumble something. Then he'll sit down and drink his morning cup of tea as if nothing had happened. I know my son!"

Vinetta smiled. It was an exaggeration, but not too far from the mark.

"I think I had better go and lie down for a couple of

hours," she said. "If everything is to be back to normal in the morning, it'll pay me to have a rest whilst I can."

Soobie slept uneasily on the settee in the lounge. It was comfortable enough and the room was much more homely than the library at Comus House, but the travel through the night and the speed with which everything had happened left him with a feeling very much like jet-lag . . .

The kidnap on Tuesday night, the escape on Wednesday, the spies on Thursday, Albert's return on Thursday evening to take them home. It had all happened with dizzy speed, as if the months of misery had collapsed into a black hole and were swirling around and around.

When morning came – Friday morning – could it really just be Friday? – Soobie woke before daybreak, sat up on the settee and switched on a table-lamp. The clock on the mantelpiece said six-thirty-five. He had slept for no more than two hours. He looked round the room and felt a surge of contentment. There would be time enough for sleeping later.

"We're home," he said out loud. "I thought we'd never make it." His whole being was filled with thankfulness for their safe return. By evening of this very day the country boys would be lighting their bonfire on Tidy Hill.

Albert came down, bleary-eyed, at seven-thirty. He had a quick breakfast and then looked in on Soobie.

"Everything all right?" he asked.

"Fine," said Soobie. "Wonderful, Albert. Couldn't be better."

"I'm going now," said Albert. "I won't be seeing you for a week or so. There are so many things I have to catch up on. My sleep for a start! But don't worry, I'll be back. If there's anything really urgent, you know how to get in touch."

Vinetta did go to bed, but she could not sleep. She was as excited as a child. Her own kitchen, her own hall, her own territory . . . and all her family safe and sound! There were so many things she wanted to do she could hardly wait for morning. And when morning came she was so exhausted she fell fast asleep. It was Tulip who welcomed Joshua home from work and made him a pretend cup of tea in the old brown tea-pot.

"Vinetta's still in bed," she said, in a deliberately neutral tone of voice to hide the smugness she was feeling. "She's been through a lot, Joshua. But then we all have. I can't help feeling sorry for her. She hasn't got much stamina."

Joshua didn't answer. He went straight to the lounge after 'breakfast'. If Vinetta was exhausted, he would not disturb her.

It was ten o'clock before she came down, looking guilty at having slept so late. Joshua, undemonstrative Joshua, put one arm awkwardly round her shoulder.

"Glad to be home?" he said.

"Words couldn't say how glad," she replied. They sat in the kitchen and Vinetta told him all about the last days at Comus House and about Soobie's terrifying time there.

"Even before the kidnapping it was terrible, Josh. Soobie went into a depression so deep I thought he was going to die."

"He'll be all right now," said Joshua. It was the longest contribution he made to the conversation.

"Yes," said Vinetta. "I think he will."

Vinetta took to herself all responsibility for Soobie's

215

rehabilitation. And the first necessity was to get him something to wear.

So, on Friday afternoon, Vinetta went shopping. She always had her emotional priorities right, whatever Tulip might say. Soobie had asked for a tracksuit. The striped suit he was wearing was beyond redemption. Yes, tomorrow might be soon enough. Tomorrow would be easy. Tomorrow was market day. Today the market was just rows of empty stalls. But Vinetta would not wait another day. However difficult it might be, she would have to go to Peachum's and buy her son new clothes. That was a priority.

She put on her hooded anorak, her fur boots, her gloves and her blue-tinted spectacles. Then, with no word to anyone, she set out resolutely towards the town centre. She thought of Hortensia who was so skilled in being unobserved. She thought of Appleby, and the time she had taken the twins right into Santa's Grotto.

These people passing me by, brushing my shoulders, are not interested in each other. They are not interested in me. One foot in front of the other. Step, step, step. Resolutely to the swing doors of the town's largest emporium. She had been there before, of course, but not often. She felt much more at home in the open-air market.

From the racks of clothes she chose a blue tracksuit with white trim. It had a zip fastener at the neck and a generous, fleecy-lined hood. Vinetta gasped when she saw the price, but she decided to pay it. Soobie was worth every penny, though she had some doubts about whether the tracksuit was! The clothes in the market were considerably cheaper.

The price of the grey trainers and the bulky grey leather gloves was not quite such a shock. Vinetta took her purchases to the square counter with the confusing PAY HERE sign right in the middle.

"Come round here, please," said an assistant in a squawky voice. "I'm on this till."

"I was here first," said a fat fur coat elbowing Vinetta aside. Vinetta kept her hood on and her head down. The fat fur coat made her purchases and strode away.

Vinetta anxiously put her things on the counter. One assistant was operating the till. Another folded and packed. Vinetta cautiously removed one glove to count out the notes needed to pay the bill and delicately accepted and pursed the change. At the end of the counter she picked up the bags. And that should have been that.

She just reached the rails at the outer door when she felt a tap on her shoulder. It was all she could do not to drop her bags and run off like a shoplifter caught in the act.

"You forgot your trainers, madam," said the girl with the squawky voice.

"Thank you," said Vinetta in a voice that would hardly emerge from her frightened throat.

To be out in the street after that was exhilarating. She had done what she had set out to do!

"Where have you been?" asked Tulip as Vinetta walked in the door carrying green plastic bags with PEACHUM printed all over them.

"Just buying some new things for Soobie," said Vinetta. "He needed them."

On that Friday evening, as soon as it was dark enough, Soobie went out jogging in his new outfit. This was done openly, but the secret Soobie had another thought in mind. They were all home again. He could not have explained why he wanted to thank the unknown God, but it seemed a fitting thing to do.

He passed the church that was always closed and due for

demolition. He noted that the Victorian letterbox had already been replaced with a stumpy thing with a hook on top. This in turn would no doubt be removed to another spot when, if ever, the road was built in its revised location. Efforts were already being made to have the old church designated a Listed Building. It was being suggested that perhaps the new road could by-pass Castledean entirely.

The second church was open and some youngsters in Scout uniforms were going in. That worried Soobie. He could only go into any church when there were very few who could see him and none who would actually look. He reached the small door of the third church and found to his relief that it was its usual quiet, early evening self. Soobie went in. Upstairs in the balcony the organ was playing softly. Choir practice. But the choir, minding their own business, were safely out of sight.

Soobie knelt beside the statue of the mother and baby and said his prayer of thanks. The mother looked loving and pleased and proud. The lively baby in her arms had his hands held out towards the world. He looked as if he were about to leap out of his mother's arms. And she looked capable enough of holding him, but confident enough to let him go.

In the balcony above, the choir was practising a morning hymn. Soobie heard the booming voice of the choirmaster saying, "Let's try to make it a bit more joyful. It's not a dirge, you know!"

The choristers sang the verse again.

Soobie, who had spent forty years reading anything and everything, recognised John Keble's words:

"Through sleep and darkness safely brought
Restored to life and power and thought."

And we have been, thought Soobie as he got up to go back home, we have been. His faith was still the faith of honest doubt. He would never know what he really believed. But he was once more Soobie the steadfast, Soobie the loving, Soobie who never let go.

As he jogged home he heard the noise of fireworks. He saw rockets shooting up high into the sky and bursting in a shower of brilliant sparks. The night was joyful. Happiness was possible. Even for a blue rag doll.

42

Albert Returns

Life at 5 Brocklehurst Grove became beautifully normal again. Miles away on Tidy Hill, a scarecrow was burnt on the bonfire. Miles away in Durham, Albert caught up on his work and his sleep.

"It's over a fortnight since Albert left and we haven't heard a word from him," said Tulip to Magnus one morning as she went through the ritual of opening his curtains and fluffing up his pillows. "I'm a bit surprised really. I mean to say, he still has our Range Rover. And there are a few things I would like him to do for us."

Magnus glowered at her.

"We can do without Albert," he said firmly. "We did without him for forty years. He was more bother than he was worth anyway."

"That is totally unfair," said his wife. "He gave us a home when we needed one. He brought us back safely when everything was sorted. He fought to save Brocklehurst Grove."

"He did next to nothing," said the old man. "The Fryers saved Brocklehurst Grove — or maybe that Caxton woman with her letters to the *Guardian* and the *Times*. The best Albert could do was write to the *Castledean Gazette*!"

"It was Albert who started the campaign," protested Tulip. "The others just followed."

"Appleby started it," said Magnus. "The petition was her idea. That young man would have given in without a shot fired if it hadn't been for Appleby."

Tulip looked at him severely.

"I'm not going to talk about it whilst you're in this mood. You're twisting the truth. And whether he helped or he didn't, he still has the Range Rover and we paid for it."

On this point, Magnus was much more generous than his wife.

"Albert has it," he said, "and Albert can keep it. We don't need it now. And it's all in his name anyway."

"It cost a lot of money," said Tulip. "I think we should still have the use of it. Or maybe we could sell it."

Magnus sat bolt upright in his bed and gave Tulip a look of exasperation.

"You dare to criticise me for saying what is no more than true, and now it is you who are being mean and paltry. Albert, I still maintain, was fairly useless. But he did his best and I don't begrudge him the car."

That was almost the final word on the matter.

Albert put in an appearance the very next day. The Range Rover drew up at the front gate. Number 5 Brocklehurst Grove had no garage, but the drive was broad enough for a vehicle and the double wrought-iron gate gave easy access.

Poopie and Wimpey saw Albert arrive and rushed to open the gates for him.

"We haven't seen you for ages," said Wimpey excitedly. "We thought you weren't coming back."

Poopie said nothing, but did his usual tour of the Range

Rover and had to be persuaded to leave it and come into the house.

"I've brought the car back," said Albert to Tulip when he went to see her in the breakfast-room. "It's the first chance I've had. What would you like me to do with it?"

"Well," said Tulip, "Sir Magnus and I have discussed the question. We think it is only fair that you should keep it. It is yours now, yours entirely. There may be one or two things you could do for us, very occasionally, where having a car might be useful even in town."

Albert was grateful but uncertain. The gift seemed disproportionately large. He said doubtfully, "Are you quite sure? It cost a lot of money. I could probably sell it for you."

"We are quite sure," said Tulip with just a twinge. "If it will make you feel any better you can pay us something for it after you sell Comus House. There's no hurry."

"It'll never sell," said Albert. "Nobody wants it."

"Of course somebody will want it," said Tulip crisply. "Every house has its buyer. What have you done so far about selling it?"

"Well," said Albert, "I had an agent in shortly after my parents died. He valued it and put it on the market. I suppose it is still on the market, for that matter."

"What happened?"

"There hasn't been a flicker of interest," said Albert. "To be perfectly honest with you, that house is a millstone."

Tulip looked puzzled.

"Two years on the market and nobody even looks at it. Did they advertise, these agents of yours?"

"I had to pay for the advertising," said Albert sheepishly, "and I couldn't afford much."

"Who are the agents?"

"Tothill and Whymper," said Albert, pleased to be able to

give a respectable answer. Everybody in Allenbridge knew Tothill and Whymper.

"Never heard of them," said Tulip.

"They have a shop on the main street in Allenbridge, just round the corner from the marketplace. They're quite well-known."

Tulip shook her head and sighed.

"Albert Pond! You're not fit to be let loose. I know more about the world out there than you do! You're a hopeless case. Do you know that?"

"Yes," said Albert. "I suppose so."

He hadn't the least objection to being called a hopeless case in such a motherly voice. It made it seem a friendly thing to be.

"Very well then," said Tulip. "Let's consider what you should do. First, we must find you a reputable auctioneer to dispose of the contents of the house – Christie's perhaps. Some of those things might be a lot more valuable than you seem to think."

Albert nodded. It was nice to have somebody making decisions for him again. He never spoke of his parents' death. He could hardly bear to think of it even now. It was an event that had left him not only sad but stranded.

"When the house is cleared," Tulip continued, "put it into the hands of a really big estate agent that has a department specialising in large country houses. Let them do whatever advertising they consider necessary. Any settlement can be made after the house is sold. I'm not saying you will be wealthy when it is all complete, but you won't be scraping along the way you are now."

Tulip spoke with knowledge and authority. Like Appleby, what she was not born knowing she made it her business to find out. Though Tulip's sphere of interest was somewhat different. She was the only rag doll in the world to read the *Financial Times!*

Before Albert left, Tulip made another arrangement with him, one to please her daughter-in-law.

"You can bring the washing machine down from Comus House before you do anything else. It will easily fit in the back of the car. And you can get a plumber to fix it up in our kitchen just as you did before. It's not fair to ask Vinetta to go back to using the old twin-tub."

43

Poopie and the Rabbit

It was a wet, wet day in the middle of December. Poopie prowled round the house feeling bored and frustrated. Everybody was doing something. Wimpey was making yet another outfit for her doll. Appleby and Pilbeam, for some reason best known to themselves, had gone up to the attic.

"No, you can't come," Appleby had said when he tried to tag along. "We don't want you. Go and play with your Action Men."

Poopie had kicked the skirting board and shouted, "I don't want to play with them. They're just toys. I'm bored, bored, bored, bored, bored!"

"I reckon little brother is bored," Appleby had said in a heavy drawl that sounded a bit like Wimpey's American doll. It was an accent she loved to copy.

Pilbeam looked disapproving.

"Leave him alone, Appleby," she said. "You're as bad as he is."

And they left him alone, getting himself into a worse and worse mood. It was not that he was growing out of Action Men. He never would really. It was just that on this particular day he wanted to be out in the garden and that was impossible. The rain was lashing the window panes and drumming on the conservatory roof. Poopie's thoughts turned, as they often did, to Andy Black.

He's probably back in the stable, he thought, looking for me. Weather like this, he's sure to be sheltering. I wish we'd never left Comus House.

That was not exactly true either. Like all the Mennyms, he loved Brocklehurst Grove. He loved Castledean. And, unique among the Mennyms, he knew how to settle anywhere. But on this particular nasty wet day, he felt stymied.

He went down to the kitchen. Vinetta was putting clothes into the automatic washing machine.

"Wonderful, isn't it?" she said. "I thought when we left Comus House that I would never see it again. I expected to go back to struggling with the twin-tub. I can't believe how lucky I am!"

Poopie looked furious.

"It's all right for you," he said. "*You've* got what *you* want."

Vinetta turned her full attention towards the indignant ten-year-old.

"And what do you want, Poopie?" she asked gently. A less tolerant mother would have lost her temper. Vinetta, as always, waived the right to be angry.

"I want Andy Black," said Poopie. "If you and Granpa hadn't stopped Dad making a hutch for him he wouldn't have been able to run away."

"You'll feel better when the rain stops," said his mother. "Why don't you play with your Action Men? You can take them into the conservatory for a change if you like."

Poopie scowled and said nothing.

"Tell you what," said Vinetta, "I'll have a word with your father. Maybe we can get you a pet rabbit some time."

Poopie faltered. It went against the grain to show any interest when he was in such a bad mood.

"It wouldn't be Andy Black," he said, but it was clear that he would not be at all averse to the company of another rabbit. Vinetta was as good as her word. But when Joshua, Tulip and Sir Magnus himself all, for a variety of reasons, gave the thumbs down to the possibility of buying a real live rabbit, she had to come up with a compromise.

The compromise was ready a few days before Christmas.

"You can have this now," said Vinetta, pleased with her efforts. "It can be an early present."

She had taken a large cardboard box to Poopie's room. It was about the size of a portable TV set and it was all wrapped up in shiny red paper.

"What is it?" asked her son eagerly. He had been in the middle of a game with Hector, Basil and Co when his mother tapped on the door. But a shiny red parcel was definitely worth stopping for!

"I'll leave you to open it," said his mother. "I hope you like it."

Alone in his room, Poopie pulled off the paper and opened the box. There inside was a furry rabbit, light grey with dark grey inside its large ears. Its eyes were pink beads and it had very realistic whiskers. The ears unfortunately drooped to either side of its head giving it the appearance of a cross between a rabbit and a basset-hound.

Poopie took one look at it and went into a full-scale tantrum.

"What does she think I am? A baby? What do I want with a cuddly toy? A nasty, rotten cuddly toy!"

Soobie was in his own room sorting out some books. He heard the thudding and the thumping and the howls of rage and went over to investigate.

"Hold on, Poopie," he said as he went into the room just in time to see his brother fling the rabbit into the corner. "What's up with you?"

"It's her," he said. "She's stupid. She's made a daft rabbit and expects me to play with it. I'm ten years old, not ten months."

"There is a difference," conceded Soobie, "but Mum's done her best. You shouldn't be so ungrateful."

He went to the corner and picked up the rabbit. It was beautifully made, with a strong potential for being real.

"Try talking to it," said Soobie, "and stroking its head."

He remembered how he and his mother had talked and talked to Pilbeam till she came to life.

Poopie scowled.

The rabbit had a scared look in its pink eyes.

"You're as daft as she is," said Poopie. "And it doesn't even look like a proper rabbit. I've never seen a rabbit with ears like that. You could almost tie them under its chin."

Soobie, with a flash of inspiration, remembered a phrase from a book he'd once read.

"You could think of it as a special kind of rabbit," he said. "Your own special rabbit, made especially for you."

"Don't talk wet," said Poopie. "It's a soppy cuddly toy and I don't want it. You might as well give it to Googles."

Soobie looked very stern.

"You will do no such thing. Mother made that rabbit for you. You're a self-centred, ungrateful brat. Our family's full of them. I sometimes wonder why Mum doesn't give up trying."

"Well, what did you think of your rabbit?" Vinetta asked hopefully.

"It's all right," said Poopie. "I suppose I'll get used to it. But it's not Andy Black."

"It couldn't be, sweetheart," said Vinetta. "It was the best I could do."

Poopie put the rabbit on a stool in the corner of his room and ignored it.

44

Return to Comus House

Albert's visits to Brocklehurst Grove became increasingly frequent. He stayed over at weekends. He saw less and less of his former friends and more and more of the Mennyms. He played chess with Soobie. He argued with Appleby. With Pilbeam he read poetry. He even told stories that kept Poopie and Wimpey still for at least half-an-hour at a time. And always and always he confided in Tulip. The valuation of his property, she decided, should be made in mid-January.

"No good bothering before the holiday. Let the new year shake the creases out of its coat first."

The house should be kept at least as clean as it had become during the sojourn of the Mennyms.

"Get your Mrs Briggs to give it a going over once a week. You can take her there and back. Give her a bit extra for travelling time – but not too much. She is competent, I hope?"

Tulip had eyed him sharply as she asked the question. Albert was perfectly capable of employing an incompetent housekeeper.

"She's very thorough," said Albert. "You should see her cleaning the cooker top."

That was good enough for Tulip. The times they had cooked for Albert made her well aware of how dirty a cooker top could become.

"You'll spend Christmas with us," said Vinetta. "We'd all like you to. I'll get you one of those frozen dinners you enjoy so much."

Albert agreed.

So he had to turn down a very tempting invitation from Lorna's mother, Jennifer Gladstone. A real Christmas dinner with a real family. It would have made a wonderful change from a pub lunch with a couple of bachelor friends – last year and the year before – and it would have been, he had to be honest, more appetising than anything Vinetta might manage to make. However, a promise is a promise.

The late invitation came after Albert kept *his* promise to Lorna. On the last Thursday of term, Jennifer Gladstone came into Durham with her daughter. They had coffee in the Union with Albert and from there they set off for Comus House.

Mrs Gladstone – Jennifer, do call me Jennifer – was a nice fluttery woman. She was not as down-to-earth as Vinetta and much less calculating than Tulip. Her fair hair was very fine and never quite tidy. Her blue eyes watered easily. If there was any resemblance between her and her daughter, it lay in bone-structure rather than colouring. They both had long-ish faces and firm chins. They were both a little above average height and quite slim. Lorna's dark eyes and black hair came from the Gladstone side of the family.

Jennifer enjoyed the trip to Comus House. She had visited only once before and that was when she was really too young to remember. The only thing that seemed at all familiar inside the house was the jug with the little boy climbing up to steal the nest.

"I remember that," she said, delighted. "It is the only thing I do remember. Isn't that marvellous? I must have been no more than three when I saw it."

Albert thought about the auctioneer due to come in January. On impulse, he said, "You can have it, Mrs Gladstone, Jennifer. I'm sure you'll treasure it."

"Oh, no! I couldn't possibly. It's yours."

Jennifer in a flutter was as bad as Miss Quigley had been in her cupboard days. Lorna stepped in and said, "For goodness' sake, Mum, Albert really wants you to have that jug. Take it and say thanks. We'll have to find something to wrap it in for the journey home."

Albert gave her a smile of gratitude.

"Come to us for Christmas dinner," said Jennifer. "It'll be noisy – Lorna's the oldest and the quietest, but even she can do her share. The rest of them have to be heard to be believed. But the food will be good, I promise you, and you might find it fun to be in the middle of a bear garden!"

"Sorry," said Albert. "I really would love to come, but I've already promised to spend Christmas with some friends of mine and I can't let them down."

"New Year maybe? Come for New Year's Day instead," said Lorna.

"Lorna!" said Jennifer. "Don't push. Albert has lots of friends, I'm sure. He might not have time to come to us."

"I have got time," said Albert. "I'd really love to come – if you're sure you'd want me."

"Albert Pond!" said Lorna, exasperated. "Stop being so diffident. It must be a family trait. Thank goodness I've missed out on it! Yes, Mother, he does want to come. Yes, Albert, we do want you."

Her smile took the edge off her words. Albert laughed a

little nervously. Jennifer fluttered slightly. But it was settled that he should be their guest on New Year's Day.

"Come New Year's Eve and see the new year in," said Lorna. "You can sleep in Robert's room. He's going to stay with a school friend straight after Christmas. You needn't even drive yourself. Dad and I will come and fetch you. I'll give you a ring to remind you we're coming."

From Comus House they drove on down to Castledean where Lorna and her mother asked to be set down in the High Street to do some Christmas shopping.

Albert drove past Brocklehurst Grove on his way out of the town. He was tempted to call in, but there was still another day to go before term really ended. So he passed on by.

45

The Christmas Presents

Sir Magnus decided to break the habit of a lifetime and come down to the lounge for Christmas Day. After all, he had travelled as far as Comus House with no ill effects. So he descended the two flights of stairs and prepared to preside over the Christmas festivities. Soobie helped him and Tulip watched them anxiously. Sir Magnus clutched the handrail with his right hand. His left arm was draped over Soobie's shoulder and in his left hand he carried a totally redundant walking-stick which waved about in the air. It was not an easy undertaking. It would be even more difficult taking him back up to bed, but Albert would be there to give an extra hand. They had done it before and managed perfectly well.

Everyone was delighted to see the head of the household sitting in Joshua's armchair and looking singularly benign. Poopie and Wimpey could not have been more pleased if Santa Claus himself had come. He was wearing a maroon-coloured velvet jacket with a tie belt round the waist and a pair of dark green tartan trews. His purple feet could just be glimpsed above his green leather slippers.

"You look great, Granpa," said Poopie. "Really great."

It set the tone for the day – all love and friendship.

They did not go into the dining-room for Christmas dinner. Sir Magnus had never pretended to eat a meal and the others were afraid he might be embarrassed. They all stayed in the lounge and exchanged presents.

Among the grown-ups, the only present of any general interest was the large package brought in by Miss Quigley.

"This," she said, "is my present to everyone. I hope you'll all like it."

She took it near enough to Sir Magnus's chair for him to reach out and pull one end of the shiny red ribbon that was tied into a big bow in the middle of the rectangle. That ceremony over, Poopie and Wimpey were allowed to remove the wrappings, which they did most unceremoniously, ripping the paper off with all speed and no dignity. It was, of course, a painting.

Everyone looked at it in amazement. It was the largest picture Miss Quigley had ever painted. It showed moorland and fields stretching for miles and miles under a pale sky of yellow and turquoise. Narrow roads wound up to the horizon and a gentle, misty sunset.

"It's the view from Comus House," said Pilbeam. "You've done it beautifully, Miss Quigley."

"And all from memory," said Hortensia proudly. "I left my sketches behind when we returned."

"It is a very fine piece of work, madam," said Sir Magnus. "Very fine indeed."

"It was a beautiful place, you know," said Miss Quigley, glowing at the praise. "We'll never see such breadth and majesty again. I wanted to remember it. I'm sure that in some strange way we all miss it."

Come off it, thought Soobie, we couldn't get away from it fast enough. Yet under the cynicism there was a twinge of regret, a feeling of nostalgia for something left behind.

"It was a good place to visit," said Tulip, "but not a place to stay."

They all felt more comfortable hearing her say this. It gave them the right to have pleasant memories of their stay in the country.

Appleby's biggest present was a guitar. She was delighted with it. It was the first time in all her years that she had ever been given a musical instrument.

"Will you be able to play it?" asked Poopie doubtfully.

Appleby gave him an exaggerated look of superiority and proved her point by managing to strum the strings quite convincingly.

Pilbeam was very pleased with her CD player. The stereo she shared with Appleby was in Appleby's room and played only the music that Appleby liked – undiluted pop! Pilbeam yearned for a more varied diet. Now in her own room she would be able to listen to the music she wanted.

For Soobie there was a beautifully illustrated copy of Lord of the Rings and another dark blue tracksuit identical to the one he now wore. It was, Vinetta thought, a very small step in the right direction. Next year she might even risk buying him one in a different colour.

Poopie was given a box full of Lego bricks that included a couple of motors worked by batteries.

But the present that vied with Miss Quigley's for beauty and interest was Wimpey's. On a base of blue cardboard waves, three feet square, was a perfect luxury liner.

"You've given her a boat," said Poopie disapprovingly. "That's not fair. Girls don't like boats."

"It's not a battleship, you know," said Vinetta smiling. "It's a cruise liner. It makes a change from dolls' houses. Your father made it for her."

And he had. Every bit of the liner from the stem to the

stern, from the gangplanks to the hammocks on the sundeck had been made by Joshua in secret in his spare time. There was a ballroom with crystal chandeliers. There was a restaurant with tables and chairs. And the whole side of the ship was hinged at the bottom so that it could be lowered to reveal all the parts inside – the galley, the engine room, the bar and the cabins on two decks.

The passengers and crew were jointed dolls bought from Peachum's, but their clothing had been made with loving care by Vinetta.

At one o'clock, Albert Pond arrived. Vinetta took his dinner out of the oven and he ate it at the kitchen table where he was well used to eating by now. It was a 'Turkey Dinner for One' but he still enjoyed it. Vinetta had even managed to provide a glass of real wine. She kept him company whilst he ate. The others remained in the lounge.

After his meal, Albert distributed the presents he had brought and was given books and stationery and handkerchieves in return. From Miss Quigley he received the long-promised portrait in its carved and gilded frame. Then they all sat and talked and helped the young ones to play with their toys till it was dusk. Poopie and Wimpey, helped by Pilbeam and Soobie, took their presents away to their own room. Miss Quigley carried Googles off into the nursery. Then the rest of the family settled back to enjoy a quiet evening. They closed the curtains, but decided against switching on the ceiling lights. The two table-lamps were lit. The standard lamp gave a soft glow to the round table in the corner.

Sir Magnus was still in Joshua's armchair. Appleby was sitting cross-legged on the hearthrug, quietly strumming her guitar. At the round table sat Albert and Pilbeam, close together, looking at the poetry book he had bought for her.

"Let me read you this one," he said. As he began to read, the hush that often falls on desultory conversation became one of deliberate, pleasurable listening. Even Appleby ceased to pluck the strings of her guitar.

He read the words as if he already knew them by heart:

"Had I the heavens' embroidered cloths,
Enwrought with golden and silver light,
The blue and the dim and the dark cloths
Of night and light and the half-light,
I would spread the cloths under your feet:
But I, being poor, have only my dreams;
I have spread my dreams under your feet;
Tread softly because you tread on my dreams."

When he had finished, the room was filled with a silence so charged that everyone was searching their minds for a way to break it. But no one knew how.

Vinetta it was who said, a little too late for comfort, and in a voice that was not quite on key, "That was lovely, Albert."

But the spell was not broken. The silence was even more powerful than before. Soobie looked across at his twin sister and came awkwardly to the rescue.

"Poetry is dangerous stuff," he said. "If you go too near the edge, you might fall in!"

Albert laughed and the others joined in hesitantly, though some of them did not quite understand the joke. But the spell was broken, and that was the main thing.

"I think it is time I went to bed," said Sir Magnus. "I have some papers I want to read before I sleep."

It was a relief to help him up, to be busy, to draw as far away from the edge as possible.

"Albert Pond is falling in love with you," said Appleby as

she sat in front of her dressing-table mirror brushing her hair. She said it in a slightly mocking, sing-song voice, clearly fourteen not fifteen, and nowhere near sixteen.

"Don't talk rot," said Pilbeam sharply. "He is a human being. I am a rag doll."

She got up abruptly from the chair by Appleby's bed.

"If you're going to talk like that," she said, "I'm going straight to bed. I'm tired anyway."

"I'm sorry," said Appleby. "It was just a bit of fun. I didn't mean to vex you."

She looked at Pilbeam anxiously. The apology was clearly meant and behind it there was even a glimmer of understanding.

"You haven't vexed me," said Pilbeam, relenting. "I am going, though. I really do feel very tired."

She went to her own room, holding herself stiffly, feeling like a tightly-wound spring. Then she lay on her bed in the darkness and sobbed inside because things were not, could not, would never be, different. Soobie's twin – oh, yes, she was that all right. They were definitely two of a kind.

46

Paddy Black

On Boxing Day, Poopie was sitting in his own room making an ocean liner with Lego bricks. If Joshua could make one with wood and nails, making one with Lego must be easier. It would take patience, but Poopie had patience when it came to things. It was only people that made him lose his temper.

What were intended as small wheels, Poopie easily converted to use as portholes. The two motors he would fix up in the engine room and eventually he would be able to have his boat moving round the room, not just standing still on a piece of choppy cardboard pretending to be the sea.

He might even be able to give the ship a rolling motion if he used a combination of large and small wheels underneath it.

"There," said Poopie as he fixed on a funnel, "how do you like that, Droopy Lugs?" He looked triumphantly across at the toy rabbit. Poopie had grown quite fond of it really, but it was not something he would ever tell anybody. They would think it was sissy.

"Can I have it?" said Wimpey.

Poopie looked up to see his twin standing in the doorway.

"What a cheek!" he said. "What a blooming cheek! They give you a boat that has absolutely everything and then you have the nerve to ask for the one I've made."

"I don't mean your boat, silly," said Wimpey. "I mean the rabbit."

She looked longingly at the furry creature that had stayed uncuddled in the corner.

"No, you can't have it," said Poopie. "It was made for me."

"I've never seen you play with it," said Wimpey.

"I don't play with it, stupid," said Poopie. "I wouldn't be so daft. I pretend he's alive, like Andy Black was."

"Same difference," said Wimpey.

"No it's not. It's a proper pretend, like drinking tea, or when Mum makes cakes, or Dad smokes his pipe. This is my rabbit," said Poopie, "and he's called Paddy Black."

"But he's not . . ." began Wimpey and stopped as she realised that they had had that conversation before. The last time the rabbit was brown and furry. This time it was grey and velvety.

"It's not quite the same as having a real rabbit," said Poopie. "I won't be able to feed him properly. But we can have terrific pretends."

Willing as ever to contribute ideas, Wimpey said, "I know how we could make him hop. Really hop. We'll get some elastic from Mum's workbox and tie it round his middle."

The word was the deed and, in less than a minute, the twins were up on the landing, bouncing Paddy Black over the bannister. What began as a perfectly respectable pretend turned into a hilarious children's game. They let the elastic unwind from the card, dropping it and then jerking it back till the rabbit was bouncing vigorously in the stairwell. Finally, they managed to make it bump its tail on the carpet in the hall below. It fell with anthropomorphic fear. It radiated surrogate joy.

"It's the highest-hopping rabbit in the world!" yelled Poopie.

At that moment, Granny Tulip came up the stairs, on her way to see Granpa.

"I'll take that," she said, holding out one hand.

Poopie looked as if he were about to say something outrageous. Wimpey interrupted in time to say, "Granny means the elastic, not the rabbit."

Poopie untied it and handed it over, all tangled. Tulip took it without another word. She had other things on her mind.

Wimpey picked up poor, maltreated Paddy Black and cuddled him. Poopie, overcome with jealousy, seized the rabbit and, hugging it to his chest, ran off to his own room. He slammed the door behind him. The game was over. Wimpey was not welcome.

47

Magnus Speaks to Albert

"I shall have to speak to him," said Sir Magnus ominously.

"Albert?" said Tulip, knowing well where his thoughts were leading. She was sitting in the armchair beside the bed.

"Who else?" said Magnus frowning. "He's giving my granddaughter some very odd notions. I don't want her made miserable longing for the moon. What right has he to come here and upset everybody?"

Tulip let pass the unfairness of that question. She knew what Magnus really meant — Pilbeam, the sweetest and most reasonable of his grandchildren, must not have her heart broken.

"Send him to me," he said. "Let's get it over with."

"He's leaving the day after tomorrow anyway," said Tulip. "He's spending the New Year with friends of his — other friends. Let's just leave it at that."

"He'll be back," said Magnus grimly. "He'll always be back till he's told very firmly that we don't want him."

"Tomorrow then," said Tulip. "Tell him tomorrow. It has been such a happy holiday. Let's not spoil it."

Sir Magnus grunted but agreed. Tulip went about her

work and left him with his desk across his knees and his bed strewn with books and papers.

When Vinetta came up half an hour later, Magnus was still brooding.

"Has Tulip told you?" he asked.

"About Albert? Yes, she has. And I think you're right. I wouldn't want Pilbeam to grow too fond of him. He's bound to leave us some time. Better sooner than later."

Vinetta was soft in most things, but if her children looked like being hurt she could be totally unfeeling and completely ruthless.

Sir Magnus looked at her kindly.

"You're a good woman, Vinetta," he said. "No one could care more for their family than you do. And they don't always descrve it."

As Vinetta was about to leave, Magnus said, "Tell Albert to come and see me at eleven o'clock tomorrow morning. I won't discuss it with Tulip any more. She has too much of a soft spot for that young man. Where is he now, by the by?"

"He's taken Appleby and Pilbeam for a drive down to Durham. It'll be their last outing, I suppose," said Vinetta a bit sadly. "They said they'd be back before dark."

This time they were. Albert was given his summons and wondered what it foreboded.

Next morning, at eleven o'clock prompt, he presented himself at Sir Magnus's room. He tapped timidly at the door before entering.

"Come in, Albert," said the old man. "Take a seat. We shall have to have a talk."

Albert sat down on a stiff-backed chair.

Tulip came purposefully into the room, knitting in hand, and sat in her usual armchair.

Magnus gave her a look of disapproval. Why could she not have stayed downstairs in the breakfast-room or busied herself elsewhere in the house? She was never there when she was wanted. Why couldn't she make herself scarce now?

"This was intended to be a tête-à-tête between Albert and me," he said pointedly.

"That's all right," said Tulip. "Just pretend I'm not here. I'll get on with my knitting."

Her tight little smile deterred Magnus from any further protest. He turned his black button eyes and his full attention on Albert who was sitting on the edge of his chair and looking very nervous. Magnus made no attempt to conceal the purple foot but Albert was so concerned at whatever it was the old man was going to say next that he did not even notice it.

"There are certain things we must get clear, Albert," Magnus said slowly. "You are not a foolish young man. You appear to have your fair share of good sense. Good sense should tell you that we do not need you now. The Grove is saved. We are home again. You do not belong here. It will be much better for you and for us if you return to your own world and leave us to get along in ours."

Tulip turned the page of her knitting pattern noisily.

Albert looked from one to the other.

"I don't see it like that," he said. "I enjoy being here. You have all become part of my life, and I thought I was part of yours. I help whenever I can. The Range Rover is useful to you in all sorts of ways."

Tulip's crystal eyes gleamed. The Range Rover was useful, definitely useful. But even she knew that it was something they would have to learn to do without.

Sir Magnus sighed and raised himself higher on his pillows.

"I see I shall have to be brutally frank. We do not need you and we do not want you."

Albert blushed.

Tulip looked annoyed.

Sir Magnus gave her a sidelong glance and began to work himself up into a fury. She knew the score. She knew what had to be done. What right had she to look vexed at this stage?

He turned his full wrath on the unfortunate Albert.

"You are no use to us at all, Albert Pond. If the truth be told, you never have been. You created a panic that didn't exist. You dragged us up to Comus House and then dashed us back again, a totally unnecessary, ridiculous excursion. How plain do I have to be? You are not wanted."

Albert's brown spaniel eyes stung with the threat of tears. Rage? Hurt? Embarrassment? All of these things. The old man's judgement on the trip to Comus House sounded uncomfortably near the mark. It was a twisted interpretation, a being-wise-after-the-event, but it had some validity. They both forgot Appleby's role in pushing the business on. They both forgot the glare of publicity that had surrounded the saving of the Grove. And, being wise after the event, they both ignored the fact that it could have gone the other way. The Grove could still have been demolished.

"I did my best," said Albert. "I only did what Aunt Kate asked of me. If it was not the right thing, then she is the one to blame, not me."

"Do you think I really believe all that balderdash about you seeing a ghost? I don't believe in ghosts," said Sir Magnus, with scant regard for logic. "I never have."

It was Albert's turn to grow angry.

"I don't see why you shouldn't," he said, raising his voice for the first time ever in that house. "You're pretty incredible yourself. A rag doll. That's what you are. A rag doll with purple feet. Just remember that. A helpless old rag doll with no knowledge and no experience of the world outside these four walls."

"No knowledge! No experience!" shouted Magnus. "No one in this house has less experience than you. We all have a forty years' start on you — forty years or more! As for the car you keep on about — take it. We don't need it. We did without one for long enough. We can do without one again."

Magnus quivered. Tulip gave Albert a look that warned him to be silent. It was, as always, a look that calmed him. He stood up and in a quietly dignified voice said, "I'll get my things together and go. When I have sold the Range Rover, I'll send you a cheque."

He passed Appleby on the landing but did not even see her. Tulip did.

"Listening at doors, madam?" she said tartly. "Is that another of your accomplishments?"

"I didn't have to listen," snapped Appleby. "They were shouting loud enough to be heard all over the house."

Tulip gave her a withering look and hurried on after Albert.

48

Tulip Talks to Albert

Albert was in Soobie's room, packing his weekend bag. His heart was much nearer breaking than Pilbeam's had ever been.

Tulip came in behind him.

"Come to the breakfast-room, Albert," she said. "I have to talk to you. My husband's behaviour was disgraceful, but he had his reasons. When you are finished here, come and see me."

Albert looked up, shamefaced.

"I shouldn't have said all those things," he said.

"You were provoked, Albert. Terribly provoked. I understand that. Come down and we'll talk it over."

Tulip was sitting at her desk when Albert came in. She motioned to him to sit in the armchair.

"Sit back. Be comfortable," she said. "This is not an inquisition."

Albert did as he was told.

"My husband can be very harsh," Tulip began. "He should have explained things better."

"But you want me to go too?" said Albert, hoping that

she would give him the comfort of saying no, even though his going was now inevitable.

Tulip felt very sorry for him, but she had to be honest.

"You do have to go," she said, " – for your own sake, never mind ours."

Albert looked about to protest but Tulip fixed him with a glance.

"Go back to Durham," she said. "Mix with your own people. That is your real world. This is all illusion. You cannot fall in love with a rag doll, Albert, and she must not fall in love with you. That is why Magnus was getting himself worked up. That is why he so distorted the truth about the help you gave us. I don't know why he couldn't bring himself to be more straightforward – to say that you must go away and forget us for Pilbeam's sake. But that is the truth."

Albert said awkwardly, "I love all of you, even him."

"I know," said Tulip. "I know. But you are a human being with a future in the world of human beings. You will fall in love and marry one of your own kind. That is the way of things."

Tulip said no more and waited for Albert to speak.

"Nothing can be as simple as that," he said. "My knowing you isolates me from the rest of mankind. If I tell, it is a betrayal and I doubt if anyone would believe me anyway. If I don't tell, I create an enormous barrier between myself and any other human being."

"It won't be like that," said Tulip with a sudden clairvoyance. "When you leave this house today, you will forget that we exist."

"I will never, never forget you," said Albert fervently.

"You will, Albert," she said. "I don't know how, but it seems to me that that too is in the nature of things."

"What about the car?" he asked. "Will that turn into a pumpkin?"

Tulip shrugged.

"I don't know," she said. "I just have the deep conviction that someone, somewhere, has the power to make you forget."

49

The Departure

Everyone gathered outside the front door to see Albert leave. Only Sir Magnus and Pilbeam were missing. With the exception of Tulip, and the ever perceptive Appleby, no one knew how final that parting would be. But they knew it was a different sort of departure. Albert accepted his exile but still did not believe that he would really forget the Mennym family.

"I won't be coming back," he said quietly to Soobie. "Your grandfather wants a clean break. But that doesn't mean I can't write to you. We can play chess by post."

Soobie gave him a long, a silent, look before saying, "I'll wait for you to make the first move." But he knew, he knew, that Albert never would write, that this was the end of their friendship.

Wimpey gave Albert a hug and said, "You will come back some day, won't you?"

"If I can," said Albert.

Poopie said a very brief goodbye. He was anxious to get back to his room where the cruise liner was making excellent progress and the rabbit was lodged in a hutch he had made for him.

Miss Quigley, with Googles in her arms, stood well back in the doorway and encouraged the baby to wave her hand.

Tulip and Vinetta came out and fussed over Albert, making sure that he was wrapped up warm. Tulip put a scarf she had knitted around his neck.

Appleby said regretfully, "No more drives in the Range Rover." She remembered that the scooter was still in the garden shed and she hoped that everybody would forget about it. A motor scooter might well come in handy some day.

"Where's Pilbeam?" said Wimpey suddenly. "She hasn't come to say goodbye."

"She's probably busy," said Vinetta quickly.

"She can't be too busy to say goodbye to Albert," said Wimpey and before anyone could stop her she raced off into the house and ran up the stairs.

"Pilbeam, Pilbeam, come now or you'll miss Albert," she shouted. "He's going away and he might not be back for a long time."

Pilbeam *was* busy. She was sitting on the floor sorting out her new CDs. It was a deliberate effort to shut Albert out of her thoughts. Appleby had told her all about the quarrel between him and Granpa. She felt as if her innermost dreams had been trampled underfoot.

Looking at Wimpey, who was standing there impatiently, Pilbeam could think of no way out of saying goodbye. Steeling herself for the ordeal, she got up and followed her sister down the stairs.

"So you're going," she said to Albert. She tried to sound very cool and grown-up. She almost succeeded. "We'll miss you. We've had lots of fun. Even Comus House was an experience worth having – something to look back on."

"Your grandfather has decided that I must go away and

stay away," said Albert in a voice that only Pilbeam heard. "This is not of my choosing."

Then on an impulse he kissed her cheek. "Goodbye, Pilbeam. Goodbye," he said.

The black button eyes that had learnt to see suddenly did something they had never done before. They cried real tears. Just a drop or two, easily brushed away, but real. Pilbeam made sure that no one saw them, not even Albert. He got up into the driving seat of the car and briefly grasped hands that reached out in a final farewell.

After the car had left the drive, Joshua closed the gates and they all went into the house. Only Appleby and Pilbeam lingered. They stood in the garden long after the car was out of sight.

The day was cold and overcast.

Pilbeam sighed.

"He'll never come back," said Appleby gently. It was an unusual tone of voice for Appleby, but not completely unknown.

"I know," said Pilbeam. "Do you not think I know?"

"Please, please, Nuova Pilbeam," said Appleby, seeing the sadness in her sister's face, "let's go inside and pretend something else – something happy."

They went back into the house together, and together they listened to music in Appleby's room.

50

The Last Word

When Albert drove out of Brocklehurst Grove he forgot the Mennyms completely. Once and for all and finally he forgot their very existence. The past was changed especially for him. It was a small concession in the history of the universe, a mere drop in the sea of infinity. On a cosmic scale it was a tiny, tiny miracle, but certainly no party trick. It took much more power than the spirit of Kate Penshaw could ever possess! She knew that, and she trembled.

The car's log book showed that it had only ever had two owners and they were both called Albert Pond. The bit of his memory that had been full of rag dolls suddenly became flooded with knowledge of Eric the Red, on whose explorations Albert was to become a world authority. It was as if the episode with the Mennyms had been no more than a dream.

But it wasn't a dream. It was a real experience and no experience can be completely lost. The heart stores what the head forgets. So what did he really remember? The love he had truly felt for Pilbeam was ready there as a pattern for loving. The joy and comfort he had felt as one of a family was imprinted on his soul as a model for his own family life with children and grandchildren in the century to come.

On a more mundane, practical level, he had an exact idea of how to sell Comus House and all its contents! That was something not erased from his memory.

In the weeks and months that followed Albert's departure, all of the Mennyms settled back into what they hoped would be a beautifully normal life. Noisy. Yes, they would always be noisy. But under the noise, peaceful and untroubled by the world outside. That was all they asked of life. That was all they had ever hoped for. Especially Vinetta. If she could have wrapped her whole family safely in the cloths of heaven, she would have done so.

As for Pilbeam — her heart soon mended. She was only sixteen. At sixteen, hearts break and mend quite easily. Pilbeam never forgot Albert, but the memory, oh the memory, was sweet.

Don't miss MENNYMS UNDER SIEGE, the next book in the series, now available from Julia MacRae Books, price £9.99.

From Mennyms Under Siege

"I need a fringe."

Pilbeam was gazing at herself critically in a mirror propped up on the kitchen table. Her long black hair was combed back from her broad forehead. Her mother, busy ironing, looked up from her work and smiled.

"Need? Surely you mean 'want' or 'would like'?"

"No," said Pilbeam. "I do mean need."

Vinetta stood the iron on its heel and went and sat down beside her eldest daughter.

"Well, come on. Explain yourself," she said. "It's not like you to use the word 'need' so carelessly."

"I need a fringe," said Pilbeam, "to hide my brow and to act as a sort of disguise for the outside world."

That was a fair enough reason, but obviously not the complete story.

"You've managed well enough so far," said her mother. "What is different now?"

"I want to go to the theatre," said Pilbeam. "Really go to a real theatre. I will be sitting next to *people*. I need my face to be as veiled as possible by my hair."

Her hair reached nearly to her waist. It was thick and

heavy and looked completely genuine. Pilbeam was the family beauty, like the princess out of a fairy tale. And the Mennyms were a strange family, a family of life-sized rag dolls created forty-four years before by Kate Penshaw, a lonely old lady whose hobby became her passion in life. After her death, the dolls had come mysteriously to life and taken over Number 5 Brocklehurst Grove, living there almost as if they were human. Except for Pilbeam. She was the last of Kate's creations and had lain unfinished in the attic for forty years. Soobie, her twin, had found her in a wicker chest and Vinetta, her loving mother, had finished the work that Kate had long ago begun.

The taking over of Kate's house had been surprisingly easy. Her heir, Chesney Loftus, had failed to come from Australia to claim, or even inspect, his inheritance. Among Kate's papers the Mennyms had found the name of an agent to whom they had written claiming to have been Kate's paying guests, and asking to be allowed to remain on as tenants of the property. Chesney himself had died three years ago, leaving the house he had never seen to what he must have assumed to be his aging tenants, for however long Sir Magnus and/or his son Joshua should reside there. He would clearly not have expected them to live forever. On their demise, the property was to go to an English branch of Kate's family.

In the forty-four years of their residence, the Mennyms had never found it difficult to come and go to the shops and the market and the park. It was simply a matter of wearing clothes to cover cloth, and dark glasses of various styles to hide button eyes. But this going to a theatre was different. How different, Vinetta was not sure. She was startled at the thought of her daughter being in such close proximity to people, but she respected Pilbeam's wishes and trusted her judgment. It was her deeply held belief that one should not be constantly frustrating the young.

She looked closely at Pilbeam's hairline.

"If I combed your hair forward," she said, "I suppose I could cut some of it into a deep fringe for you."

"No," said Pilbeam, "that wouldn't do. It might make a line across the top and it would thin the hair down. I want more hair on top, not less. You could try making a fringe and stitching it into place. Then if ever I didn't want it we could unpick it, like Dad's beard when he was Santa Claus at Peachum's."

"What would I use to make it?" said Vinetta. "Your hair is so beautiful and silky. It would have to be an exact match. There's nothing suitable in my workbox. I know there's not."

"No problem," said her daughter. "Just cut a few inches off the bottom. I have often thought it was a bit too long at the back."

The transplant was performed that very afternoon. Poopie and Wimpey, the ten-year-old twins, came and watched, fascinated. It was a frosty January day with lowering clouds threatening snow. The twins were bored enough to welcome the distraction of seeing their elder sister suffer. It was not painful, of course, just irritating and restricting. Pilbeam was not at all pleased that her two younger siblings were such earnest spectators.

"It must feel funny," said Wimpey as she watched the needle going in and out on Pilbeam's brow. She stood with her head on one side, looking up at her mother and sister. Wimpey's pale blue button eyes were always full of wonder. Her golden curls, tied in bunches with satin ribbon, made her look old-fashioned and even more doll-like than the rest of them.

"Hold still," said Vinetta when Pilbeam turned her head

to look at her sister. "I don't want to get the thread in a tangle."

Joshua, their father, coming into the kitchen after his nap, raised his eyebrows and then took refuge in the brown teapot, pretending to brew tea in it and pour it out into his old mug. He was a quiet man, his dollness well hidden beneath a gruff manner. Like all the family, his life was a mixture of reality and pretence. He really did work as a nightwatchman at Sydenham's Warehouse. He really did tend the garden at home, helped by his son Poopie. But the pipe he 'smoked' was a pretend. The 'tea' he brewed was make-believe. There really is a football team called Port Vale, one of the oldest in the English League, but Joshua, their lifelong supporter, had never been to see them play.

When she had finished fixing the fringe in place, Vinetta stood back to admire her work. Then she held one mirror in front of Pilbeam and another behind to let her daughter see her hair from every angle. The twins watched her.

Poopie looked up from under his own yellow fringe, cut straight across his brow, bright blue eyes glinting. "I don't like you with a fringe," he said. "I liked you better before."

Pilbeam looked at herself anxiously.

"What do you think, Dad?" she asked Joshua.

"Not much different," said her father, barely raising his eyes from the newspaper he had begun to read.

"Well, I think it looks lovely," said Wimpey.

Miss Quigley came in to collect a bottle for Googles, the baby. For the past three years, she had been nanny to Vinetta's youngest child. Before that she had 'lived' in the hall cupboard, appearing in the Mennym house at intervals as a visitor and Vinetta's friend. Her own home was supposed to be in Trevethick Street, but that was just a pretend. She was a lady of uncertain age with a plain but pleasant face and thin hair tied in a tight little bun on the back of her neck. Since moving properly into the house, she had developed talents, not only as a nanny but also as an artist painting pictures that, had she been human and not a rag doll, would surely have led to her work receiving wide acclaim. She took one look at Pilbeam and smiled a tight little smile.

"Snow White has turned into Cleopatra," she said as she passed by.

Pilbeam looked annoyed, and Vinetta, seeing the expression on her daughter's face, knew just what was coming next.

"It must look odd," said Pilbeam. "We'll have to unpick it."

"Take your time," said her mother. "Think about it. Get used to it. Remember, it was your idea in the first place. And did you say you *needed* a fringe."

Vinetta was reluctant that her work of the past two hours should be completely wasted. She wished dear Hortensia had been a little more tactful. It was nothing to say really, no insult to be likened to the Queen of Egypt, but young people do take things so seriously. Pilbeam suited her new hairstyle. Anyone with any taste could see that. And after a day or two they all did.

"It makes you look older," said Granny Tulip. "More grown up."

"I *am* more grown up," said Pilbeam.

It was Tuesday, and she and Tulip and Vinetta were sitting in the breakfast-room, which was Tulip's office in this house that was home to three generations. Lady Tulip Mennym was an amazing woman. With her white hair and her blue-checked apron, she looked a typical, housewifely granny. She was small and neat and quick in speech and movement. But in addition to this, she was an excellent businesswoman.

And, as if that were not enough, she was so skilled at knitting that the most famous store in London sold the garments she designed and made. Harrods, naturally, was never aware that the firm of 'tulipmennym' was so different from any of their other suppliers.

There was something in the tone of Pilbeam's voice that made her grandmother look up, shrewd crystal eyes showing an awareness that Pilbeam was making a real statement and not just uttering empty words.

"In fact," Pilbeam went on, "I have decided to be eighteen instead of sixteen. Soobie agrees. Since last year, we have moved on. The whole family has. But, in our case, it meant more. We were adolescents. Now we are grown up."

Vinetta said anxiously, "Eighteen or sixteen – there's little difference. We are as we are. And, whether we like it or not, our circle is complete. In the human world, change is con stant. Children grow up and get married and grow old. That sort of cycle is not possible for us. We wouldn't want it anyway. We do well enough as we are. In more than forty years we have never grown any older. There are many in the world outside this house who would envy us."

It was less than a month since their one and only contact with a human being had been finally severed. Albert Pond, Kate Penshaw's great-nephew, had been called upon by the ghost of Kate to save the Mennym family when their home at Number 5 Brocklehurst Grove had been threatened with demolition to make room for a motorway. With the excep tion of Sir Magnus, everyone in the family came to look on Albert Pond as one of themselves, an honorary rag doll, but his departure became essential when he seemed to be falling in love with Pilbeam, and she with him.

Pilbeam smiled at her mother, poor, worried Vinetta,

whose sensibilities made it difficult for her to find the right words.

"It's all right, Mum," said Pilbeam. "I know I'll never have a boyfriend. I don't think Granny could knit me one! Growing up, being mature, means accepting what you are and. making the most of it. Soobie has changed too, you know, Mother. He has learnt to enjoy life more, even as a blue rag doll, jogging secretly through the dark streets. Maybe it's the tracksuit that's done it!"

Soobie, Pilbeam's twin, was unlike every other member of the family, for he was completely blue from head to foot and his eyes were bright, shining, intelligent silver buttons.

Vinetta looked pleased at Pilbeam's words about the tracksuit. Vinetta had bought it at Peachum's, the town's biggest department store, when Soobie's old, striped blue linen suit was in tatters and he had at last agreed to wear a more modern, more human, style of clothing.

"I think you're right," said Vinetta. "Soobie really does look smart in a tracksuit."

Pilbeam laughed.

"That was a joke, Mum. Why do you always have to take everything so literally?"

Vinetta smiled.

"Part of my nature, I suppose. I am a bit too set in my ways to move on very far."

"Well, I'm not," said Pilbeam. "So take it as a fact. I am eighteen years old. And so is Soobie. We are not children."

"Where does that leave Appleby?" asked Granny Tulip.

At that moment, Appleby appeared in the doorway. The fifteen-year-old was very vivacious, with red hair and green eyes. She was the most volatile member of the family, a perennial teenager who never told the truth when a lie would do.

"What about Appleby?" she asked, sounding cross and suspicious.

"Appleby is Appleby," said Pilbeam. "She'll never be any different."

"I don't want to be," said Appleby. "That fringe has gone right to your head!"

Pilbeam held her breath and did not laugh. Vinetta got up to go.

"Let's leave Granny in peace now. She has her work to do, and so have I."

After they were all gone, Tulip, following the careful directions Pilbeam had given her earlier, rang the booking office at the Palais Majestic. She had felt a bit unsure at first of the wisdom of the venture, but Pilbeam was so certain and so determined that her grandmother had not argued.

"I'd like one seat in the stalls for *The Merchant of Venice* on Thursday, twenty-seventh January," said Tulip when her call was answered.

"One moment, please," said the girl on the other end of the line. Voices could be heard talking to each other in the office. Then the girl returned to the telephone and began, "We have. . . ."

"It must be on a side aisle, near an exit," Tulip interrupted.

"No problem," said the girl. "Seat 33N is exactly what you require. We'll post the ticket out to you, if you would like to give me particulars of your credit card . . ."

So it was all arranged. Pilbeam, a week come Thursday, was to have her first ever visit to the theatre. A real, happening-now thing, not a fictional memory. . .

Other great reads *from* **Red Fox**

Further Red Fox titles that you might enjoy reading are listed
on the following pages. They are available in bookshops or they
can be ordered directly from us.

   If you would like to order books, please send this form and
the money due to:

ARROW BOOKS, BOOKSERVICE BY POST, PO BOX 29,
DOUGLAS, ISLE OF MAN, BRITISH ISLES. Please enclose
a cheque or postal order made out to Arrow Books Ltd for the
amount due, plus 75p per book for postage and packing to
a maximum of £7.50, both for orders within the UK. For
customers outside the UK, please allow £1.00 per book.

NAME_____

ADDRESS_____

_____

Please print clearly.

Whilst every effort is made to keep prices low, it is sometimes
necessary to increase cover prices at short notice. If you are
ordering books by post, to save delay it is advisable to phone to
confirm the correct price. The number to ring is THE SALES
DEPARTMENT 071 (if outside London) 973 9700.

BESTSELLING FICTION FROM RED FOX

☐	The Present Takers	Aidan Chambers	£2.99
☐	Battle for the Park	Colin Dann	£2.99
☐	Orson Cart Comes Apart	Steve Donald	£1.99
☐	The Last Vampire	Willis Hall	£2.99
☐	Harvey Angell	Diana Hendry	£2.99
☐	Emil and the Detectives	Erich Kästner	£2.99
☐	Krindlekrax	Philip Ridley	£2.99

PRICES AND OTHER DETAILS ARE LIABLE TO CHANGE

ARROW BOOKS, BOOKSERVICE BY POST, PO BOX 29, DOUGLAS, ISLE OF MAN, BRITISH ISLES

NAME ....

ADDRESS ....

....

....

Please enclose a cheque or postal order made out to B.S.B.P. Ltd. for the amount due and allow the following for postage and packing:

U.K. CUSTOMERS: Please allow 75p per book to a maximum of £7.50

B.F.P.O. & EIRE: Please allow 75p per book to a maximum of £7.50

OVERSEAS CUSTOMERS: Please allow £1.00 per book.

While every effort is made to keep prices low it is sometimes necessary to increase cover prices at short notice. Arrow Books reserve the right to show new retail prices on covers which may differ from those previously advertised in the text or elsewhere.

BESTSELLING FICTION FROM RED FOX

☐	The Story of Doctor Dolittle	Hugh Lofting	£3.99
☐	Amazon Adventure	Willard Price	£3.99
☐	Swallows and Amazons	Arthur Ransome	£3.99
☐	The Wolves of Willoughby Chase	Joan Aiken	£2.99
☐	Steps up the Chimney	William Corlett	£2.99
☐	The Snow-Walker's Son	Catherine Fisher	£2.99
☐	Redwall	Brian Jacques	£3.99
☐	Guilty!	Ruth Thomas	£2.99

PRICES AND OTHER DETAILS ARE LIABLE TO CHANGE

ARROW BOOKS, BOOKSERVICE BY POST, PO BOX 29, DOUGLAS, ISLE OF MAN, BRITISH ISLES

NAME ....

ADDRESS ....

....

....

Please enclose a cheque or postal order made out to B.S.B.P. Ltd. for the amount due and allow the following for postage and packing:

U.K. CUSTOMERS: Please allow 75p per book to a maximum of £7.50

B.F.P.O. & EIRE: Please allow 75p per book to a maximum of £7.50

OVERSEAS CUSTOMERS: Please allow £1.00 per book.

While every effort is made to keep prices low it is sometimes necessary to increase cover prices at short notice. Arrow Books reserve the right to show new retail prices on covers which may differ from those previously advertised in the text or elsewhere.

BESTSELLING FICTION FROM RED FOX

☐ Blood	Alan Durant	£3.50
☐ Tina Come Home	Paul Geraghty	£3.50
☐ Del-Del	Victor Kelleher	£3.50
☐ Paul Loves Amy Loves Christo	Josephine Poole	£3.50
☐ If It Weren't for Sebastian	Jean Ure	£3.50
☐ You'll Never Guess the End	Barbara Wersba	£3.50
☐ The Pigman	Paul Zindel	£3.50

PRICES AND OTHER DETAILS ARE LIABLE TO CHANGE

ARROW BOOKS, BOOKSERVICE BY POST, PO BOX 29, DOUGLAS, ISLE OF MAN, BRITISH ISLES

NAME..

ADDRESS..

....

....

Please enclose a cheque or postal order made out to B.S.B.P. Ltd. for the amount due and allow the following for postage and packing:

U.K. CUSTOMERS: Please allow 75p per book to a maximum of £7.50

B.F.P.O. & EIRE: Please allow 75p per book to a maximum of £7.50

OVERSEAS CUSTOMERS: Please allow £1.00 per book.

While every effort is made to keep prices low it is sometimes necessary to increase cover prices at short notice. Arrow Books reserve the right to show new retail prices on covers which may differ from those previously advertised in the text or elsewhere.

Join the RED FOX Reader's Club

The Red Fox Reader's Club is for readers of all ages. All you have to do is ask your local bookseller or librarian for a Red Fox Reader's Club card. As an official Red Fox Reader you only have to borrow or buy eight Red Fox books in order to qualify for your own Red Fox Reader's Clubpack – full of exciting surprises! If you have any difficulty obtaining a Red Fox Reader's Club card please write to: Random House Children's Books Marketing Department, 20 Vauxhall Bridge Road, London SW1V 2SA.